The Famous Stanley Kidnapping Case

The Famous Stanley Kidnapping Case

by Zilpha Keatley Snyder

FRONTISPIECE BY ALTON RAIBLE

A YEARLING BOOK

Published by
Dell Publishing Co., Inc.
1 Dag Hammarskjold Plaza
New York, New York 10017

Yearling ® TM 913705, Dell Publishing Co., Inc.

ISBN: 0-440-42485-2

Reprinted by arrangement with Atheneum Publishers
Printed in the United States of America
First Yearling printing—November 1985
CW

The Famous Stanley Kidnapping Case

one

None of it would have happened if it hadn't been for Molly's Italian uncle, so the very beginning was way back in February. David remembered the beginning very well, because for just a minute, it had scared him half to death.

It all started on a cold drizzly afternoon when he and Amanda had been, as usual, in the midst of some kind of an argument. They'd gotten off the school bus together and walked down the long curving driveway that led around to the back of the big old house and, still arguing, slammed through the back door into the kitchen—and found Molly crying at the kitchen table.

The crying, by itself, wouldn't have been too much of a shock, because Molly tended to cry quite a bit for an adult person. David had seen her cry over a burned dinner—which was the way Molly's dinners turned out fairly often—or because she'd messed up a painting she'd been working on. But that was red-faced, angry crying that usually got mixed up with laughing at herself for being so ridiculous. This was different. When Molly's face came up off her arms, it looked terrible: pale and swollen and awfully sad; and immediately David felt himself going stiff and cold with fright. Amanda, however, was so busy winning the argument that she didn't even notice until David said, "Molly?" in a shaky whisper. When Amanda finally looked at her mother and said, "Mom? What is it? What happened?" she sounded surprised and worried, but even then not really scared. Not the way David was.

It wasn't until later, when he'd had time to think about it, that David understood the difference. He decided then that Amanda's reaction was only natural—but so was his. Probably most people who were thirteen years old, like Amanda, just naturally felt that really terrible things only happened to other people—in the newspapers or in some other town or country. So even when she saw Molly's face and knew something bad had happened, she wasn't really frightened. David, who was actually almost a year younger than Amanda, would probably have felt the same way, except that his own mother had died when he was nine years old; and after something like that happens, you're just not as sure anymore. So when he'd first seen Molly's face, he hadn't been sure that something hadn't happened to—Dad, maybe, or one of the kids.

But then Molly said it was her uncle—that Uncle Sid had died in Italy—and suddenly David felt as if something huge and cold in the middle of his chest had broken up into warm trickles of relief. Which would have been a good feeling, except that right away he started feeling guilty for being so glad about Molly's poor old uncle. Particularly when Molly was obviously feeling absolutely terrible about him.

All the Stanley kids had heard quite a bit about Uncle Sid since the summer before when Molly had married Jeffrey A. Stanley, who was their father. Uncle Sid had been an artist like Molly, and a bachelor with no family of his own to take an interest in; so when Molly was a kid, he'd been almost a second father to her, teaching her about painting and giving her lots of advice about what she ought to do. He'd always been crazy about Italy and spent part of every year there, so Molly always called him her Italian uncle, which he really wasn't, since Molly and all of her relations were more Irish than anything else. But for almost as long as Molly could remember, Uncle Sid had been telling her she should go to Italy to paint and study art. He had told Molly that she had a tremendous amount of talent, much more than he had, but that she would never get to be a great artist and fulfill her destiny if she didn't go to Italy, which was the birthplace of art and culture and civilization and nearly everything else that you could think of. He'd kept on urging her to go, even offering to help with her expenses, until she decided to get married to Bryan Randall, Amanda's father. That had been a long time ago, almost fifteen years, and soon afterwards Uncle Sid had moved to Italy for good. He went on writing to Molly, though, scolding her for wasting herself and her great talent and telling her that she should never have gotten married. Eventually she must have started agreeing with him —or at least, as she'd told David once, she agreed that she shouldn't have married a wheeler-dealer Hollywood PR man—and so finally she'd gotten a divorce. Uncle Sid had been very pleased when he heard about that, and he'd started urging her to bring Amanda and come to live in Italy. But then, when he heard that Molly had gotten married again, and this time to a college professor with a whole ready-made family, he'd finally given up entirely—in disgust, Molly said.

But now he was dead, and Molly hadn't realized just how much he meant to her until the telegram came that afternoon. After she told David and Amanda about it, she put her head back down on her arms and cried again with huge shivering sobs, like Janie at the end of a tantrum. Except you could do something about Janie, such as ignoring her or whispering to somebody so that she had to shut up to listen. But Molly's crying was different, and there wasn't anything David could do except stand around feeling helpless and try not to let Amanda see his face. Not that he was crying about somebody he'd never even met. It was just that Molly's crying seemed to be catching—like when someone yawns. Fortunately Dad came home not long afterwards, and David was glad to let him take over the job of cheering Molly up.

For a few days Molly wasn't herself at all, very quiet and preoccupied. Dad must have noticed it,

6

because he got everyone, including Amanda, together and gave a lecture about how Molly was going through a difficult time and needed peace and quiet, and how everyone could help. And how he'd better not catch anyone being uncivilized or else he might forget himself and resort to some old-fashioned negative reinforcement.

They all nodded. Janie and Esther and Blair happened to be sitting side by side on the loveseat, and they all nodded and went on nodding, like a bunch of birds on a telephone wire. Looking at them —the twins weren't quite five yet, and Janie, who was very small for her age, wasn't much bigger—you might think they wouldn't understand what Dad meant. But they were used to the way he put things, and besides, all kids understand what a sentence that has "or else" in it means, at a very early age. But as soon as Dad left the room, Amanda made a sarcastic face and said, "Negative reinforcement! La-de-dah! He never stops being Professor Stanley, does he? Not even when no one's around but kids." She motioned toward the loveseat. "Look at them. Do they know what 'negative reinforcement' means, for heaven's sake?"

David looked. You might guess by looking that Esther could be pretty one-track minded and that Blair was a little spacier than most four year olds, but Amanda ought to know by now that the way Janie looked had absolutely nothing to do with what she knew—or what she was thinking, or what she might be going to say or do next.

"We do too," Janie said. "We know what negative reinforcement means. Don't we Tesser?"

Esther nodded uncertainly, and Amanda said, "Okay. What does it mean?"

Janie rolled her eyes thoughtfully. "Negative reinforcement," she said in the tone of voice she always used when she was showing off her I.Q., "negative reinforcement is the opposite of positive reinforcement and not as nice. But it's usually just getting sent to your room, except when it's old-fashioned negative reinforcement, and then you get spanked first."

It was as good a definition as most people a lot older than seven would have come up with, but Amanda only shrugged and walked away.

Anyway, the lecture must have made a definite impression because everyone was particularly good for the next few days, or if not good, at least quiet. David and Amanda managed to have most of their arguments in places where Molly wouldn't hear them, and even Janie had an amazingly quiet tantrum when David wouldn't let her kick Blair for feeding a special strawberry she'd been saving to his pet crow. After a while Molly began to be cheerful again, and nothing more happened for several weeks. But then David and Amanda came home from school one day and found that Molly had been crying again, only this time it was different.

Molly's eyes were red, but this time she seemed more excited than sad, and she wouldn't tell them what had happened. "Not until Jeff gets home," she said. "Wait until Jeff gets home." So they had to wait, sitting in the kitchen, raising their eyebrows at each other, while Molly bustled nervously around trying to start dinner but mostly going in circles and forgetting what she had started out to do.

At last Dad walked in the door loaded down with books and papers, and Molly ran across the room and threw her arms around him books and all. "Oh Jeff," she said. "We're all going to Italy." The way Dad stared at her when he got through grabbing at falling books and papers, it was pretty obvious that he couldn't have been much more surprised if she had said, "We're all going to the moon." He went on looking surprised and puzzled for quite a while after she started explaining what she meant.

The explanation didn't make much sense at first to David, either. Just a bunch of stuff about "dear, sweet, stubborn old Sid" and how he never gave up until he got his way, and legacies and stipulations and Italian inheritance laws. But at last she slowed down and began over at the beginning, and it all started to make sense.

It seemed that Molly's uncle had left her quite a lot of money in his will, except that the money was in Italy and had to be spent there, and she couldn't have any of it unless she went there. The letter from the lawyers had come just that day, but it was easy to see that Molly had already done a lot of thinking about it. "We could rent the house, Jeff," she said. "And surely you could get a year off or at least a semester. You should have had a sabbatical years

9

ago. And we could find a villa in the country where there'd be space for the kids to play, but not too far from Rome, or perhaps Florence. Florence was always Sid's favorite. And I could paint, and you could work on your textbook. And perhaps Amanda and David could go to an Italian school and learn Italian, or if that doesn't work out there are correspondence schools. And it wouldn't matter if Janie missed a year, if it came to that, since she's so far ahead of herself already. And it really won't make much difference for the twins, since they'd only be in kindergarten. And, oh Jeff, won't it be wonderful!"

Molly wasn't standing on her tiptoes the way Janie did when she was telling something particularly exciting, but you got the feeling she was about to. For a long time Dad only nodded, looking very solemn and thoughtful. Then he asked to read the letter. When Molly got it for him, he sat down at the kitchen table and read it very slowly and deliberately, while Molly and David and Amanda stood around the table watching him. At last he put it down on the table and smoothed it out very carefully with both hands, then looked up grinning. It was suddenly obvious that he was just as excited about going to Italy as Molly was.

Dad began to talk then—about people who might be able to take over his classes and leaves of absences and sabbatical years and difference of pay leaves. And Molly brought up buying a new car in Europe and charter flights and whether to fly directly to Italy or perhaps to London or Paris first—

and it all started to sink in. David began to realize it really was going to happen, and it was a very strange feeling. The Stanley family hadn't traveled much at all since he was old enough to remember. He'd never even thought about visiting a foreign country, except maybe Mexico or Canada. But now it seemed like a very interesting thing to do. To start with, flying across the whole country and the Atlantic Ocean in a 747 would be pretty exciting; and then to actually live in a totally different country, where people spoke another language and did all kinds of things differently might be. . . .

He was just beginning to get some ideas about what it might be like when something hit him in the ribs. It turned out to be Amanda's elbow. "Bye-bye, David," she said.

"What do you mean 'bye-bye'?" he asked her.

"I mean 'bye-bye,' you're off to Italy whether you like it or not."

Dad and Molly were so busy making plans that they didn't seem to have noticed, but Amanda was staring at them with squinted eyes and her mouth pulled down in the corners, the way she used to do all the time—and still did, only not quite so often.

"Well, so are you," David said.

"Not necessarily. I could stay with my father." Amanda's father lived in a really plush apartment house right near the ocean in Santa Monica, and every once in a while she went to visit him. But usually only for a few days at a time during vacations. At first, right after Dad and Molly were married, Amanda had talked a lot about how great her father was and how crazy he was about her and how she hated Molly, and how the divorce had all been Molly's fault, and how she would rather live with her father. But things had changed after a while, and Amanda had started speaking to her mother again. Most of the time, lately, she seemed to feel okay about the rest of the family, too, including David. Most of the time, but not always.

Molly looked up suddenly and said, "What did you say, Amanda?"

"I said I could stay with my father."

Molly didn't say anything for a minute, and when she did, she didn't sound excited anymore. "You don't want to go to Italy, then?" she asked.

Amanda shrugged. "Not particularly. It's been bad enough having to change schools all the time at my age, and make new friends and everything, without having to try to make friends in a language I can't even speak."

Molly turned and looked at Dad, who was staring at Amanda with the expression on his face that always made David feel uncomfortable, whether it was meant for him personally or not.

"Well," Molly said finally, "I'll write to your father about it, but I don't know if he'll feel he can have you for such a long time. You know how busy he is."

"Yeah," Amanda said. "I know." She got up, gathered up her books and went out of the room.

David got up, too. "Where are the kids?" he asked. "Do they know yet? About Italy?"

"Upstairs, I think," Molly said. "No, I haven't told them. I wanted to be sure that Jeff thought it was a possibility first."

"Would it be all right if I told them?"

Molly looked at Dad. "Sure," he said. "Tell them. Tell them to start packing. The Stanleys are definitely going to Italy."

two

Amanda must have been listening outside the kitchen door, because when David came through it, she was just a few steps ahead of him, walking quickly toward the stairs. Halfway up she slowed down so that David caught up with her. "What did they say?" she asked. "What did they say about me after I left?"

"Nothing. I asked them if I could tell the kids about going to Italy, and they said I could. No one was talking about you."

"Oh yeah?" She went on up the stairs, but near the top she stopped again. David started to go on by her—he'd had Amanda as a stepsister long enough to know that there were times when it was best to leave her alone. And this looked like one of those times. But before he got past, she grabbed him by the back of the shirt. "Wait a minute," she said. "How soon are we going to leave? Did they say when we would be leaving for Italy?"

"We? I thought you were going to stay with your father."

"He won't let me. His new girl friend doesn't like me much."

David was confused. Amanda's head was bent down so that her long straight hair curtained her face. "Then why did you say—" David began, and then stopped. Even without seeing her face, he was beginning to get the picture. "Oh, I get it," he said.

Amanda tossed her head. "Well?" she said in a so-what tone of voice. "It served them right. They might have asked us if we wanted to go before they started to plan our lives for us. They might at least have said, 'Hey, how do you feel about moving to Italy?' before—"

"Who's moving to Italy?" Janie was hanging over the bannister right over their heads.

"We are," Amanda said before David could say anything. "The whole family. Mom's uncle left her a bundle, so look out Italy, here we come."

"Really?" Janie looked at David, and when he said yeah that he guessed so, her eyes, which were always very large and round-looking, seemed to get even rounder. "Wow!" she said, and dropping off the bannister she ran down the hall yelling, "Blair. Tesser. We're going to Italy. We're going to Italy."

Amanda snorted. "What do they know about Italy?"

"Well," David said. "Blair and Tesser probably don't know anything about Italy, but Janie—"

"Yeah," Amanda said. "On second thought you're probably right."

When they got to Janie's and Esther's room, Janie was saying, "Didn't you hear me? We're all going to Italy."

"I heard you," Esther said. "Are we going today? Can't I finish this picture first?" Esther was lying on her stomach coloring in the color book Grandma Stanley had sent her for Christmas. Molly had tried to talk her into trading it for a blank tablet because, according to Molly, coloring books stifled creativity. But Esther loved coloring books, and nobody talked her out of anything she'd set her mind on. Blair was on the floor, too, playing with his pet crow. The crow had a crayon in its beak, and Blair was holding a blank tablet—Blair was a pushover compared to Esther—in front of the crow.

"What are you doing, Blair?" David asked.

"My crow is coloring," Blair said.

Sure enough, there were a couple of straggly red scribbles in the middle of the page, but when Blair held the tablet up to the crow again, it just turned its head away.

"I don't think he's in an artistic mood," David said.

Blair sighed. "He only likes red," he said. "He won't color unless it's red."

"Then why don't you give him a red crayon? Where's the red crayon?"

"He ate it," Esther said. "He ate Blair's red and" —she reached out and tucked a crayon under her stomach—"he can't have mine."

"Listen, you guys," Janie said in an exasperated tone of voice, "aren't you excited? Don't you know anything about Italy? Italy is a very exciting place. Just wait till I tell you about Italy."

Amanda rolled her eyes and gave David a kind of "here-we-go" expression. Sure enough, Janie started in about the canals in Venice, and how everybody rode around in boats singing opera songs instead of riding in cars, and how Italians said *"chow"* all the time and *"mama mia"* and stomped around in barrels full of grapes to make wine."

"Where does she get all that stuff?" Amanda whispered, shaking her head.

"Well, you know," David said. "TV and books —and the newspapers. She reads the newspaper an awful lot for a seven year old."

"I know," Amanda said. "They oughtn't to let her."

"Who oughtn't?"

"Mom and your father. I'll bet if they asked a psychologist, he'd say that it wasn't good for her. But instead they just encourage her because everyone thinks it's just too cute to see someone so little and dumb-looking sitting around reading the newspaper. But what I think is that it's abnormal."

". . . and godfathers who tell everybody what to do and make them shoot each other, and gangsters. Lots and lots of gangsters," Janie was saying.

"See what I mean?" Amanda said.

Of course, Dad had been kidding when he told David to tell the kids to start packing because it turned out that they weren't going to leave for Italy until July, and in March that seemed a long way off. The only thing that happened right away was that Dad started bringing home all sorts of books about

Italy and, also, a set of books and records that were supposed to teach you how to speak Italian. The idea was that the whole family would study Italian together every evening after dinner. Right at first everyone was very enthusiastic, even Amanda, who seemed to have gotten over hating the idea of going to Italy as soon as she had made her point that she didn't have to go. But it soon turned out that Blair and Esther were only good for about ten or fifteen minutes of language study at a time. After that, Blair would usually go to sleep and Esther would start asking how to say words like "cookie" and "apple" and then wander off toward the kitchen. David and Amanda lasted longer, but quite often they had too much homework to do, so Janie, who learned everything faster than normal, turned out to be the only kid in the family who learned much Italian.

The hard part of getting ready to leave didn't start until June—the sorting and packing and cleaning. Everything that wasn't going to Italy had to be packed up and stored away so that the house could be left empty for the renters. For a long time Molly spent every day going through everyone's room sorting things into three piles—things that would go into storage; things that would go into trunks to be shipped to Italy; and things that would go with the family on the airplane flight. And almost every day there were emotional scenes about what things could, or absolutely could not, be left behind—such as Janie's horse collection and Esther's toy vacuum cleaner. There were also scenes about pets, like

Rolor, Blair's crow, and Velveteen, Esther's rabbit, and King Tut, who was a turkey who belonged to everyone, but mostly to Molly, who had saved his life by saying that she'd never before cooked a turkey whom she'd met personally, and she didn't intend to start. Friends had to be found who not only would keep the pets for a whole year, but also would promise to give them up when the year was over—and it wasn't easy. After a while, it all began to seem terribly complicated and an incredible amount of work, and there were times when David wondered if Italy was really going to be worth the effort.

Once when he was sitting on the floor of his closet in the midst of a pile of junk he was supposed to be sorting, he muttered, "Boy, all I can say is, Italy had better be pretty exciting." He wasn't really talking to anyone because the only other person in the room at the time was Blair, who was sitting on the window seat staring out the window. Quite often Blair didn't seem to hear what you were saying to him even if you were practically shouting in his ear, so David was rather surprised when Blair suddenly got down off the window seat and ran across the room. He stood for quite a long time just outside the closet door, looking at David with his head tipped a little bit on one side the way he always did when he was thinking. And then he said, "Janie says it is."

By then David had forgotten what he'd said so he asked, "Janie says what is?"

"Exciting," Blair said. "Janie says Italy is exciting." And then Blair said something really amazing. Of course, at the time it didn't seem particularly amazing, because it was exactly the kind of thing that Janie was always saying. But looking back at it afterwards it really was strange, because what Blair said then was, "Janie says we'll probably all get kidnapped."

three

The villa was in a part of Italy called Tuscany, a few miles from the city of Florence, and it turned out to be absolutely perfect. Everyone was crazy about it from the moment they first saw it, which was especially nice since, up until then, there hadn't been too many things about the trip that had turned out to be all that great. The airplane flight, for instance. The flight over had been one of the things that David had been particularly looking forward to, and there had been some exciting things about it—and some other things that turned out to be a pain in the neck.

One of the things that hadn't been so great about the flight was the fight that Amanda and Molly had had about whether Amanda was going to wear her Levis with the frayed-out cuffs on the airplane. Molly had won finally, with Dad's help, but Amanda hadn't been happy about it, and she certainly didn't let anyone forget that she wasn't happy. Then it turned out that their no-smoking seats were right at the edge of the smoking area, so all the smoke drifted over and gave Dad hay fever and a bad temper. Then Blair spilled his milk all over the seat and floor during dinner, and right after dinner Janie was airsick all over everything that Blair had missed. David had started out being excited about flying, but before long something, either the altitude or the vibrations, gave him a headache.

The only person who was really crazy about the whole trip was Esther, who got chummy with the stewardess and went around wearing a stewardess hat and apron and passing out earphones and pillows. The flight seemed to last forever, and by the time it was over Esther had decided she was going to grow up to be a stewardess, and every one else had had enough air travel to last for a long time.

The first few days in Italy were great. There were some very interesting things about moving into the *pensione* in Florence, which was like a boarding house run by a large Italian family in what had once been a very old private mansion. Finding an Italian car that was big enough for seven people turned out to be a kind of adventure, too. After that the sightseeing and house hunting began.

Actually the house hunting didn't take up a great deal of time because the agency that specialized in finding rentals for foreigners had such a hard time finding anything at all that was big enough for a family of seven. The rental agent who got stuck with the job was a short, wide, very excitable man named Signore Bellucci, who spoke a lot of very hard to understand English. Every morning he called Dad and talked and talked, but in the whole first week he only took the family to see two tiny apartments and a farmhouse without any heat or running water. So while they waited for Signore Bellucci to find something more suitable, there was lots of time for sight-seeing.

Everyone enjoyed the first few days. They started out at the main square, the Piazza Della Signoria, with its old palace and fountain and naked statues. Amanda and Janie had a great time giggling about the statues, especially the very famous one by Michelangelo because it was called *The David*. They all liked the Ponte Vecchio, too, the old bridge covered with jewelry shops and sleeping hippies.

And then there was the cathedral. The cathedral was—well, except for Dad, it was everyone's first cathedral, and it was certainly not like anything they'd ever seen before. Molly kept whispering, "Oh my God, Jeff. It's incredible." And everyone else seemed to be stricken speechless, which was very unusual for the Stanleys, and in Janie's case, almost a miracle.

The cathedral in Florence was their first big Italian church, but after that they saw many more, and it turned out that the whole family and particularly the little kids really got into looking at churches. Perhaps it was partly because they had never been in a Catholic church before, but Janie and the twins were absolutely fascinated by the statues and altars and candles and the beautiful frescoed walls and ceilings. And when they found out that Molly, who had been brought up a Catholic, knew who a lot of the statues were, and what was going on in all the

23

pictures, every church visit turned into story hour
Then after they became familiar with all the stories,
Janie had to tell them all over again every time they
saw another picture or statue. "Oh look, Tesser,"
Janie would say. "You remember who that is? He's
the one who . . ." And away she would go while
the twins listened wide-eyed and everybody else stood
around and waited.

Then there were the museums and art galleries.
No one had anything against art galleries to begin
with; but Dad and Molly (Molly in particular)
wanted to see an awful lot of them, and since there
was no place to leave the kids, they all had to trudge
along whether they felt like seeing any more Renaissance masterpieces or not.

By the end of the first week in Florence, what
with so many art galleries and being cooped up in
two rooms in the *pensione* when they weren't out
sight-seeing, everyone was beginning to get very tired
and irritable and very much on each other's nerves.
And then Signore Bellucci found the villa.

The villa was a huge old house in the country.
It sat near the top of a hill about a mile up from a
little village called Valle di Chiesa, and all around
it were acres and acres of vineyards, olive orchards
and forest. The villa had been the home of the Bartoli family, who had owned the land of the *fattoria*,
or farm, for hundreds of years; and although the
house had been remodeled and added to many times,
there were still parts of it that were over five hundred
years old. A small wing of the villa had been a rental

for some time and was at the present occupied by an Australian couple. Clustered around the courtyard behind the main house were several other foreign families living in houses and apartments that had once been farm buildings. Only recently, the Bartoli family had decided to move into the city to live, so now the main body of the old house was for rent, too. It would be perfect for such a fine large family, Signore Bellucci said. And as soon as they saw it, the Stanleys couldn't have agreed more.

"Isn't it wonderful," Molly said when they were on their way back into Florence in Signore Bellucci's car. "Don't you love it, kids? I know I would have adored living in a house like that when I was little." Molly turned around and looked at them—all five of them jammed together in the back seat. Blair was sitting on David, and Amanda was holding Esther. "It makes me want to be ten years old again, so I could play games about knights and dragons and captive princesses."

"It makes me want to play vampire," Janie said. She flapped her arms in spooky slow motion and bared her teeth at Esther. Esther squealed and fell over on top of Blair and David.

"Don't let her," she screamed, clutching her throat. Don't let Janie suck my blood."

After Dad finished glaring at Janie, he asked everyone for an opinion about the villa. Molly thought everything about it was wonderful, but mostly she raved about colors. "Italian colors," she said. "Why is it that in other countries ancient things go gray and grimy, but here in Italy everything manages to turn gold and cream and russet like leaves in autumn?"

Of course, Molly was always talking like that —artist talk about form and light and color—but what she said about the villa was true. Instead of being one solid color, its thick walls were a mixture of soft red-gold shades. And even where the plaster had crumbled so that the thin dark red bricks showed through, it only looked artistic—like a painting or stage set, instead of just old and worn-out.

Its age was what Dad seemed to like best about the house. He had several things to say about how people had been living in those rooms before the Pilgrims landed, and about all the famous Italians who might have stopped there on their way into Florence.

David couldn't help agreeing that there was something very intriguing about living in a house that old. He'd sat for a while on the wide window ledge in one of the strangely shaped little attic rooms, looking down at the courtyard below, and there had been something very intriguing about it. Sitting there, you couldn't help thinking about the other kids who'd probably sat there hundreds of years before. In fact, if you thought about it enough, when there wasn't anyone else around, it got almost too intriguing—like maybe someone was going to tap you on the shoulder suddenly, and when you turned around there would be this kid in tights and a tunic asking you to get off his window ledge. But when Dad asked, David only said that he thought the villa was great, and how soon could they move in.

When it was her turn, Esther said she liked the kitchen best, which was pretty predictable. Then Janie said she liked the cellar best because that's where Count Dracula lived. She lifted her lip at Esther, and then did a quick change to doll eyes and dimples when Dad turned around to glare at her. But Dad knew Janie well enough not to be fooled that easily, and he went on glaring until she said, in a phony sweet voice, "Not really, Tesser, honey. I was just kidding about Count Dracula." But as soon as Dad turned back around, she rolled her eyes at Esther and gave her lip another quick vampirish twitch.

"How about you, Blair?" Dad asked. Blair was staring out the window, and he didn't answer until Dad asked again in a louder voice. Then he tipped his head on one side, blinked his eyes slowly and after a long time he said, "Like? Best?" He blinked some more, and finally after another long wait, he said, "That lady. I liked that lady on the stairs."

For a moment that gave David a jolt because of a secret theory he'd had about Blair for a long time. Because of some things that had happened in the past, he'd developed this theory about how Blair could see and hear things that no one else could. Supernatural things. And since there hadn't been any lady at the villa, except of course for Molly, David couldn't help wondering. But then Molly said, "Oh, he means the statue of the Virgin on the landing."

And then David remembered the ceramic statue that sat in a little niche in the wall above the turn in the front stairs.

That left only Amanda, and when Molly asked her if she liked the villa she said, "Yeah. It's okay, I guess." Which for Amanda was wild enthusiasm, so it was unanimous.

There really were all sorts of things to like about the villa. There was, for instance, the huge fireplace that stretched across one end of the living room, or great hall, like a small stage. There were the two staircases—the wide marble one with the statue on the landing, and another behind the kitchen that went clear down to the cellar in a dark, narrow spiral, like the steps to a dungeon. There were the windows—all the windows in the house—that you could climb up and sit in because they were set into walls that were over two feet thick. There were the brick archways, the huge ancient-looking ceiling beams, the dark tunnellike hallways on the third floor, and all kinds of strange little nooks and crannies everywhere. Outdoors, there were a series of terraces covered with cobblestones or planted to lawn and bordered by hedges and tall, thin cypress trees. And behind the big manor house, there was a courtyard surrounded by large stone buildings that had once been barns and workshops and storage places of various kinds, but now were rentals for other foreign families. Beyond the courtyard, the dirt road wound up the hill through a wooded area and on towards a high ridge, and on either side the vineyards and olive orchards stretched away over rolling hills that climbed gradually to other high horizons. On one distant hilltop you could see what looked like a castle with turrets and towers.

That afternoon, back at the *pensione* in Florence, the whole family talked about the villa. Dad said they shouldn't come to too hasty a decision, even though their first impressions were very good, because a year was a long time and they wanted to be sure. Dad even insisted on calling up Signore Bellucci a couple of times to ask questions that had come up about schools and shopping. But by dinner time it was all decided, and the next day the Stanleys moved into the big villa on the *fattoria* above the village of Valle.

four

His first morning in the villa David woke up very early and sat in the window of his room on the second floor to watch the dawn. The hot Italian sun was still out of sight behind the eastern ridge of hills, but a glowing halo of light showed where it would soon appear.

He opened the casement window and leaned out, breathing deeply. There was a summery smell, but with a difference, a spicy tang that came, perhaps, from grapes and olives. It was very still, except for an occasional popping noise like the far-off report of a gun. Hunters probably. He'd heard about bird hunters in Italy. Squinting, he looked far up the hillside, searching among the trees for a glimpse of men with guns, but nothing moved except for a silvery stir of olive leaves in the slight breeze.

Then suddenly the silence was broken by a distant noise, an angry snarling sound that grew rapidly louder and louder. Something shiny flashed among the trees, and David's heart gave a quick extra thump of alarm. Then a swiftly moving shape swept into view on the dirt road below the forest, trailing a cloud of dust. Just as David was realizing that it was only a motorcycle, a second appeared as if in pursuit of the first. One behind the other, the two motorcycles twisted and turned down the road toward the villa, and the sound of their motors grew to a shattering roar. If anyone had still been asleep in any of the villa's houses and apartments, they were certainly awake now—awake and probably sitting straight up in bed scared to death. The two cycles flashed past the courtyard gate and roared on down the hill toward the village. The angry noise faded to a distant snarl and then died away. He was thinking about getting down out of the window to get dressed when another movement caught his eye. Something else was coming down the road.

David settled back on the ledge and waited, but these new travelers on the dirt road were moving much more slowly. It was some time before they emerged from the trees—two people on foot, making their way along the road in and out of slanting sunshine. As they came closer he saw that they were both women, or perhaps a woman and a young girl. The woman was dressed in dark colors; and the girl, who was very slender, was wearing red and had long dark hair. He watched them until they disappeared behind the courtyard wall and, a few moments later, appeared again, this time inside the gate. In the center of the courtyard they stopped and talked, the older woman gesturing with both hands and then turning to cross the yard toward the villa. David jumped down from the windowsill and started to dress. If the Stanleys were having visitors, he wanted to be in on it. He was nearly dressed when it occurred to him to look back out of the window. The pretty dark-haired girl was still waiting in the courtyard.

When David got down to the kitchen, he found Molly and Dad speaking Italian very slowly and uncertainly to a middle-aged woman with a round, smiling face and curly, gray-streaked hair. Dad had his Italian dictionary out, and now and then he would look up a word. David didn't understand most of it, but he did catch one word he knew—*mercoledi,* which he remembered meant Wednesday. *"Mercoledi,"* Dad was saying. *"Si, mercoledi. Va bene. Va bene.* Good, Good." The woman said some more things, pointing and gesturing, and then she was starting towards the door, saying, *"arrivederla"* and *"grazie,"* when Blair and Esther came in.

David was used to the way the twins intrigued people. The fact that they were the same height and age and so entirely different in every other way really caught people's attention. He had to agree that Blair was beautiful; with his enormous spacy-looking blue eyes and blond curly hair, there just wasn't any other word that seemed to fit. And Esther—Esther was round and sturdy with sleek brown hair and very red cheeks. People said Esther was cute-looking, and David guessed he agreed, except when she was being stubborn; then he sometimes thought she looked like a little bulldog. Anyway he'd seen a lot of people do a big number about how darling the twins were, and sometimes he'd wished they wouldn't. But there was

32

something about the way this Italian woman reacted that was—well—okay. She just stared at them, clasped her hands together, rolled her eyes up toward the ceiling and said some words that you didn't have to understand to know she really felt enthusiastic about kids like Blair and Esther. She went over and hugged them both before she left, and the way she did it was so natural they didn't seem to mind.

As soon as she had gone out, Molly said, "Isn't she great? And can you imagine, I'm going to have a housekeeper. Isn't that marvelous?"

"Wow," David said. "I'll say." Molly hated housework a lot. All the Stanleys had heard her say, more than once, that she was a painter by profession and a housewife only accidentally. Once when somebody said, "Don't you mean incidentally," she'd said, "No accidentally. I accidentally fell for a man with four kids." Anyway, at home Molly did a little of the housework, and the rest of the family did a little more, and quite a bit of it just didn't get done. But when Dad suggested that Molly get a housekeeper, she always said she couldn't afford it. But now things were different because the Stanleys could only stay a year in Italy and the money that Uncle Sid left was enough to live on very comfortably for a year.

"Signore Bellucci told us about Signora Lino," Dad said. "Her brother-in-law is the farmer who takes care of the crops for the Bartoli family. When her husband died a few years ago, she came here to live with her relatives, and she's able to earn a little

33

money by doing housework for the renters here at the villa. When I asked Signore Bellucci about a housekeeper, he said that no one could be better than Ghita Lino. She's already working here at the villa a couple of days a week, for the Thatchers and the English family who live in the old haybarn, and everyone seems to be very pleased with the arrangement."

"I *know* I'm going to be pleased with the arrangement," Molly said.

Looking out the kitchen window, David saw Signora Lino crossing the courtyard to where the girl in the red dress was waiting. He could see the girl more clearly now. She was, he decided, probably around fifteen years old and very pretty and Italian looking—dark and glamorous. "I wonder who that is," David said. "The girl with Signora Lino."

Molly looked out the window. "Probably one of her children. Signore Bellucci said she has quite a few."

Molly was right about the girl. On Wednesday when Signora Lino came to clean for the first time, the girl came with her again. While her mother worked in the house, she swept the courtyard and watered some planter boxes and then sat on the terrace wall reading a book. She was still there when Janie and the twins went out to play, and before long the three of them were standing around in a circle staring at her. Watching from his window, David winced. Kids were really crazy. He tried to imagine himself going right up to a strange person like that and couldn't. If he had to go out into the courtyard while the girl was sitting there, he'd probably pretend he didn't see her, or some dumb thing like that. After a while, when he looked again, Janie was sitting on the wall beside the girl, and it looked as if a big conversation was going on, which was pretty strange, considering the girl probably didn't speak a word of English. When Janie finally came back in the house, he asked her about it.

"We were talking Italian," Janie said.

David knew that Janie had done more of the recorded lessons than he had, but he also knew she couldn't possibly have learned too much. "You don't know that much Italian," he said.

"I do too," Janie said. "Besides, a lot of Italian you do with your hands, and I speak sign language very well."

Whatever language they'd been speaking, Janie certainly seemed to have gotten a lot of information. One interesting thing she'd learned was that the girl, whose name was Marzia, was only thirteen, the same age as Amanda. Which was really surprising because she looked quite a bit older. It was partly the way she dressed, he guessed, in dresses or skirts instead of Levis and tee shirts; but besides that, she was shaped more like a teenager than a skinny kid, the way Amanda still was. Janie had also found out that Marzia's father was dead and that she had four brothers and one sister and that they all lived with their uncle's family farther up the dirt road that ran past the villa.

The first few days at the villa were really fascinating. There were all kinds of explorations to go on and people to meet. Unfortunately there was only one other kid living on the Bartoli *fattoria,* a teenager, but some of the other people were fairly interesting, for adults. Actually, the teenager, Hilary Morehouse, was just about the most boring person around in David's opinion, though not everybody agreed. He lived with his parents, who were from England, in the house that was called *Il Fienile. Il Fienile* means the haybarn, but actually it was one of the biggest and nicest of the rentals. Mr. Morehouse was an ex-banker who had retired to write a book. Molly said they obviously had gobs of money. Mrs. and Mrs. Morehouse were very nice and friendly, but their son was a real oddball.

Hilary Morehouse was sixteen years old, very tall and skinny, and extremely polite and friendly in a way that made you think that if you suddenly turned into a ten-foot gorilla he'd go right on being polite and friendly without even noticing the difference. It didn't seem to David that he was at all handsome, either. He had the kind of neat, orderly-looking face that usually goes with a very thin mustache— except, of course, Hilary wasn't old enough to grow one. He went around saying things like "smashing" and "good show" in a very enthusiastic tone of voice that came off phony, except when he was talking about hiking in Italy. Then you could tell he really meant it. That summer, at the villa, he usually went around in hiking boots and Swiss-type leather shorts with about a half-mile of skinny legs in between. Except for hiking and math, he didn't seem to be at all interested in anything. In fact, he seemed to be particularly uninterested in people, which was obvious because of the way he never noticed about Amanda and Marzia. David was pretty sure that he would have noticed if he were sixteen and two girls had a crush on him, particularly if one of them looked like Marzia. As a matter of fact, he'd been noticing Marzia quite a bit already, and he wouldn't be sixteen for almost four years.

The first thing David had noticed about Marzia was her looks. But very soon afterwards he'd noticed that there didn't seem to be any particular reason why she should always come with her mother to the villa. Once in a while she helped a little with the cleaning, particularly any part of it that could be done outdoors, but usually she just sat in the courtyard and read a book. Then Janie began talking to Marzia, and it wasn't long before the truth came out. Marzia had a thing about Hilary Morehouse. And not long afterwards it turned out that Amanda had a crush on him, too. That wasn't too hard to figure. Amanda always had to do everything bigger and better than anyone else, so as soon as she found out that Marzia was crazy about Old Knobby Knees, she had to be even crazier about him.

Besides the Morehouses, the other people the Stanleys met right away were the Thatchers. They were originally from Australia, but they'd been living for several months in the small new wing of the villa.

Actually, the new wing was only new by comparison —only about one hundred years old, instead of four or five hundred. It had been built for one of the Bartolis who had been an artist, and it was mainly one enormous room with lots of windows on the north side, which was great for the Thatchers because they were both sculptors. Andrew Thatcher sculpted out of marble and granite, and his wife, Olivia, modeled out of clay. They were probably about as old as Dad and Molly, but they seemed younger—more humorous and carefree—which Dad said was because they didn't have any kids to add to the wear and tear.

But even though the Thatchers didn't have any kids of their own, they seemed to like them, particularly little ones. The Stanleys hadn't been at the villa very long before Janie and the twins were running in and out of the Thatchers' wing as if they lived there, and the Thatchers didn't seem to mind at all. Sculpting is very interesting to watch, and Andrew and Olivia didn't even insist that spectators keep their mouths shut, the way Molly did when she was painting.

It wasn't long before everyone in the family was crazy about the Thatchers, especially Molly. Molly said they were absolute darlings, and when they went so far as to offer to take care of the little kids now and then while Dad and Molly did art galleries in Florence and Siena, Molly said that other people could believe the Thatchers came from Down Under if they wanted to, but as far as she was concerned they came from Up Above—straight down from heaven. As a matter of fact there was only one thing about the Thatchers that could have been improved upon, in David's opinion, and that was the way they were so impressed by Janie.

Part of it was the language thing. Both of the Thatchers spoke fluent Italian, and they were absolutely fascinated by the way Janie was learning the language so quickly. Nobody really blamed them. People who've never had to live with a genius can't be expected to understand how they have to be treated. But after an hour at the Thatchers, being encouraged to show off her IQ, Janie usually came home and started setting everybody straight about everything, which was a special talent of hers that really didn't need any encouragement.

Besides the Morehouses and the Thatchers, the other foreign renters were: a nice old Swiss couple who lived in what used to be the carriage house; some Swedish students in the cowbarn; and a Canadian bachelor in the stable. All of the foreign renters spoke at least some English and were friendly and fun to talk to. The only really uninteresting couple lived in a very fancy cottage that had once been the pig shed. No one seemed to know much about them except that the man was from France and the woman was from America, and they obviously weren't at all interested in being friendly except to each other.

Besides the foreign renters, there were usually some Italians around the villa, too. The owners dropped by every once in a while to be sure everything was all right, and Marzia's uncle and some of his hired men were often working around the courtyard, because a few of the outbuildings were still being used to store wine and olive oil. Then, of course, there was Ghita, who came to the villa several days a week, and Marzia, who came almost as often. So it wasn't very long before the Stanleys had gotten to know a lot of new people, and probably an even larger number of people had at least heard about the Stanleys.

five

As soon as Janie and the twins got acquainted with Marzia, they started going out to talk to her every time they saw her in the courtyard, and now and then, when he had nothing better to do, David watched from a window. The more he watched, the more he thought that she looked like an interesting person. Interesting and friendly, too, at least to little kids. Several times he seriously considered going out to meet her himself, but he never quite got around to it. Part of the reason was the language thing, of course. Even in English he'd never been exactly great at striking up a conversation with a stranger, and to try it in a language he couldn't even speak seemed like just asking for a chance at the dumb-guy award of the year.

Amanda didn't go out to meet Marzia either. David wasn't sure why, because Amanda certainly wasn't what you would call a shy person; it probably had something to do with the fact that Molly kept encouraging her to do it. Molly kept saying that Marzia was just Amanda's age, and they'd probably enjoy getting to know each other very much, and that the best way to learn a language was just to pitch in and try. Amanda didn't say anything, but she didn't go out to talk to Marzia.

Then one day both David and Amanda went down to the village with Molly when she went to do some shopping. Shopping in Valle was different from shopping at home. In Valle you had to go to several little stores to get the things you were used to buying in one big supermarket. You shopped in one place for fresh vegetables, another for milk and cheese, and so forth. Most of the shops overflowed out onto the sidewalks under the arcade during the day—racks and tables in front of clothing stores, and even carcasses of animals hanging in front of the butcher shops. Molly had learned quite a few shopping words, but there was still a lot of pointing and gesturing and acting out going on, and the whole thing was a lot more fun to watch than shopping in an American supermarket.

When they got back to the villa that day, Molly let Amanda and David out of the car with the groceries before she drove on down to the parking place on the lower terrace. They were halfway across the yard when they heard Janie calling, "Hey Amanda. Come here a minute." Janie was sitting on the terrace wall with Marzia.

"Come on, David," Amanda said. "We might as well go on over and see what she wants."

"She called you, not me," David said.

"If you don't go, I won't," Amanda said, so David went, too.

When they got near the wall, Janie asked Amanda to tell Marzia how old she was. Amanda said, "I'm thirteen," and when Marzia looked blank and shook her head, she held up ten fingers and then three more.

"*Oh sì,*" Marzia said. "*Anch'io. Tredici.*"

"She says she is, too," Janie said. "Now tell her how old I am. She won't believe me."

"Janie is seven," David said and held up seven fingers.

Marzia said some surprised-sounding things. She looked at Janie and did a surprised bit by making her eyes bigger and her mouth into a circle, and they all laughed. After that they went on talking, or at least communicating, for a while about things like ages that you could do with fingers or things that were easy to act out. David had noticed that Italians were good at acting, and Marzia seemed to be especially good. She even managed to talk about the weather by acting out how hot it was. Watching her, it wasn't hard to understand how Janie had been able to get so much information in spite of having so little Italian.

They were still standing there talking to Marzia when the motorcycles went by again on the road just below the terrace wall, drowning out their voices completely with their earsplitting roar. Janie, who was crazy about motorcycles in spite of all the bad things Dad was always saying about them, jumped up on the wall to watch them go by. There were three of them this time, three guys in flashy-looking outfits, bending low over the handle bars of their shiny machines. They swept by in a split instant and disappeared up the road, leaving behind diminishing waves of sound and a swirling cloud of dust.

"Va-room. Va-room," Janie yelled, jumping up and down on the wall. When things were quiet again, she asked Marzia something in Italian, and Marzia made a face and waved her hand in a kind of disgusted gesture, as if she didn't think much of motorcycles.

Just then Molly came out looking for her groceries, so Janie introduced her, too, and Molly asked Marzia to come in for milk and cookies. From then on Marzia began to spend quite a bit of time with the Stanleys, and before long she began to ask them to go on expeditions to see interesting things in the area around the villa.

Actually, it was probably Molly who arranged the first expedition with Marzia. It happened on a very hot day when Molly was trying to paint under a tree on the front terrace, and the little kids had been interrupting her every few minutes. When noon came and Molly went into the kitchen to make lunch, Marzia was there talking to Janie, and somehow it all got arranged very quickly. It seemed that Marzia was telling Janie about a place where people had been having picnics for hundreds of years, and Molly thought it would be a great idea for her to take all the kids there for a picnic—a nice long one.

Molly fixed a huge lunch. When David said, "Wow. It's going to take us all afternoon to eat all that stuff," Molly said, "That's the general idea."

Instead of going out to the road, as David had expected, Marzia led them across the courtyard, past the Morehouses' villa—where both Marzia and Amanda found reasons to stop and talk loudly for a few minutes, but no one came out, so they finally gave up and went on—and then right up the steep hillside. Behind the villa there were two long terraces planted to grapevines and then the forest. Following a narrow path, Marzia led them to where half-ruined stone steps led from the lower terrace to the one above. On the top terrace they skirted the end of the rows of grapevine and returned to the path just where it entered the forest.

The deep shade was very welcome after the heat of the midday sun. The path wound around the side of the hill, but it was easy to see that it had once been something more than just a hillside trail. Where the hill was steep, the path had been cut back into the slope and in some places the bank had been lined with stone to stop erosion. Before long they came to a kind of decoration, a large stone urn on a pedestal. The urn was chipped and weather-stained and obviously very old. Farther on they passed two more urns and then a stone bench, curved to fit an indentation in the hillside. Near the bench Marzia stopped and began to tell Janie something about the path, but David hardly understood a word. When he asked Janie, she didn't seem too sure, either.

"About this path," Janie said a little uncertainly. Marzia says it's called a *passeggiata*. She said something about how people used to take walks here a long time ago when the family who owned the villa was very rich."

"How do you know she said that?" Amanda demanded. "You don't know all those words in Italian."

"I do too," Janie said.

"Okay, then how do you say rich? How do you say rich in Italian?"

Janie's frown turned into a triumphant grin. Obviously Amanda had happened to ask her a word she really knew. "*Ricco,*" she said in a very cocky tone of voice. "*Molto ricco* means very rich. So there!"

Amanda shrugged and walked on down the path, but Marzia poked Janie and asked something about "*molto ricco.*"

"Marzia wants to know if we're *molto ricco,*" Janie said.

David laughed. "Us? Our family? Fat chance. We're not rich."

Amanda stopped and came back frowning. "Look, David," she said, "don't answer for me, will you? *My* father is very rich, so that means I am too. If your father is rich, you are too, even if you don't happen to live together all the time."

"Okay, so you're rich," David said. "I keep forgetting." Actually, he'd heard Molly say that her first husband liked to pretend he was a lot richer than he really was, but if Amanda wanted to believe her father was a millionaire, it was all right with him.

Janie was pointing at Amanda and telling Marzia something about *"molto ricco."*

"Milionario?" Marzia asked.

"Sì. Milionario," Janie said with the doll-eyed look that could fool people who knew her a lot better than Marzia did. Marzia was looking very impressed, and there wasn't anything in the world Janie liked better than impressing people. David couldn't help grinning, wondering how Janie was going to explain how Amanda happened to be *"molto ricco"* when the rest of the family wasn't. It wasn't likely that she knew how to say words like divorce and marry in Italian. But then again, he wouldn't want to bet that she didn't. But whatever it was that Janie was telling Marzia about Amanda, the heiress, it must have been a good story because Marzia seemed to be very interested.

Janie and Marzia were still talking about Amanda when the path turned sharply and widened into a circular clearing. In the center of the clearing was a huge stone table, and all around the edges were more of the massive curved benches. Behind the clearing the hill face had been lined with heavy stone slabs, forming a high semi-circular wall. From the center of the wall water dribbled from the mouth of a gargoyle and fell into a trough below. All of the old stone—the table, the benches, the trough and the wall behind it—had once been covered with sculpted figures, but now all of the shapes were blurred by time and erosion into vague, shadowy forms.

Everyone told Marzia what a great picnic place it was, and she seemed pleased that they were all so impressed. They put the bags of food down on the table and started looking around trying to figure out where the spring was that had been piped to flow from the gargoyle's mouth, and what all the carved figures represented. All except Esther, that is, who was more interested in taking the food out of the bags and arranging it very carefully on the table.

It still wasn't very late, but after Esther had arranged and rearranged everything several times, she began to fuss about being hungry. So the picnic got underway, and while they were eating Marzia tried to tell them something about a duel. It seemed a duel had been fought right there on the picnic terrace with pistols—*"pistole,"* Marzia called them.

It was a long story, and even Janie didn't understand all of it. After a while Marzia got tired of trying to explain and began to demonstrate, and, of course, Janie insisted on getting into the act. The results were pretty confusing. According to Janie's interpretation, two men had gotten into a fight over a shopping bag and a whole lot of people had been killed, and the whole thing had happened just last Christmas. It made a good story—Esther got so excited she stopped eating for at least five minutes—but that night David found out from Olivia Thatcher that the duel had happened at Christmas about one hundred years ago. The argument had been over somebody's wife, and the one guy who got shot didn't actually die. It seemed that Janie had mixed up *"sporta,"* which means "shopping bag" with *"sposa,"* which means "wife," and then just got carried away by her enthusiasm for doing death scenes.

When all the food was finally gone, Marzia showed them a short path that led directly down from the picnic terrace to another dirt road. They all slid and scrambled down the hill and then started walking down the road, which was narrower and not in as good condition as the one that went past the villa. It led past a large quarry, where they stopped to watch some workmen loading huge slabs of stone onto a truck. The walls of the quarry formed a semi-circle of gigantic stairsteps where the slabs of stone had been cut out of the hillside. It looked as if it would be an interesting place to fool around, but all along the road there were signs that said ATTENZIONE! PERICOLO! VIETATO L'ACCESSO! in big red letters. It didn't take much Italian to figure out what that meant. A little way past the quarry, they came to where the small road merged with the larger one that went past the villa.

After that first picnic, the terrace at the end of the *passeggia* became a favorite place, not only for picnics but for all kinds of games. Janie took the twins there quite often to play medieval lords and ladies, and duels and crusades, and a game about werewolves that scared Esther so much she cried all the way home. But all the games and picnics were during the daytime. As far as David knew, nobody ever went there at night.

six

Not long after that first picnic, Marzia offered to take all the Stanley kids to the Saturday morning market at Valle. They started very early in the morning and walked down the road past the olive orchards and vineyards and the solid tile-roofed farmhouses. Marzia pointed out things and told about them, and Janie translated. Either Janie's Italian was improving rapidly, or else it was her imagination, because they all learned some amazing things about wine making and wild boar hunting that day, plus a whole lot of local gossip. When they finally got to the village and turned the corner into the piazza, they were all surprised at how different it was from weekdays.

The piazza in Valle was a large square paved with cobblestones with a statue of an Italian soldier in the center and places for parking cars all around the edges. During the week the central part of the square was empty, except for little groups of men standing around talking things over, which was something Italian men seemed to spend a great deal of time doing. But on Saturday morning the whole area was suddenly covered with dozens of little booths and stalls under bright-covered umbrellas and awnings. Some of the booths were mobile affairs on the backs of trucks, and some were just a table under an umbrella. The merchandise included everything—from fresh fish to French perfume. Everyone in town seemed to be there having a great time shopping and visiting and arguing, and the whole thing was exciting and a little like a carnival.

Marzia seemed to know everyone. People kept stopping her. They were all very friendly and curious about the Stanleys, particularly the little kids. Blair especially got fussed over and called things like *"bellino"* and *"un angelo."* But people were always saying things like beautiful and angelic about Blair, and even when it was in English he never paid any attention, so you didn't have to worry about it's being bad for his ego, the way you did with Janie.

They stayed in the village most of the morning, and Marzia took them all around the piazza and introduced them to dozens of people, several of whom gave them little samples of what they were selling; slices of cheese and salami and pieces of candy. It was a lot of fun and David was having a great time until, just as they were getting ready to go home, they ran into Hilary. After that, as far as David was concerned, the whole expedition turned into a real bore. Hilary had been shopping at the market, and he was about to leave, too, so he decided to walk home with them. From then on, David was stuck with

51

just the little kids to talk to while Marzia and Amanda concentrated on trying to impress Old Knobby Knees.

Actually Hilary seemed to be more interested in some books about Tuscany that he'd bought at the market than he was in the girls, but Marzia and Amanda both kept trying to get his attention. Once in a while they succeeded by getting him to talk about the books, which were in Italian and were all about castles and monasteries and other famous places in the area. Hilary said he could read Italian, but he didn't seem to speak it very well, which meant that most of the time he was talking in English—to Amanda.

David couldn't believe Amanda. He could just imagine what would happen at home if any member of the family tried to tell her all about some fifteenth century monastery, complete with all the facts and figures and names and dates, clear down to what the monks ate for breakfast. But here she was, hanging on every English-accented word as if she'd never heard anything more fascinating in her whole life. The twins weren't paying any attention, but Janie, who had recently added "romance" to her list of special interests, along with gore and violence, kept poking David from time to time and making significant faces about the way Amanda was acting. And, of course, Marzia noticed. Did she ever! While Hilary was talking to Amanda, Marzia looked as if she were about to explode. David couldn't help feeling a little nervous because he'd heard how Italian people take things like romance very seriously. He wouldn't have been at all suprised if something serious had happened right then between Marzia and Amanda. But nothing did, and the next time Marzia came to the villa she seemed as friendly as ever. In fact, she asked the Stanleys to go on another exploration.

"Marzia wants to take us to see something scary," Janie said; but when David asked what it was, she didn't seem to know for sure. "I don't know exactly," she said. "But it's up the hill a long way, and it's something about dead people."

The next morning Marzia arrived at the villa dressed for serious hiking, in blue jeans and a pair of heavy boots that looked too big for her. She was carrying a plastic bag with some salami sandwiches in it. She pointed to the bag and said some things in Italian.

"Marzia says we'll be gone a long time and we'd better take some lunch," Janie translated. David was starting the lunch when Amanda came downstairs, and when Marzia saw that she was wearing sandals, she shook her head and made a lot of gestures and acted out stumbling and hurting her toe.

"She says you'd better change your shoes," Janie said.

Amanda gave Janie an icy stare and said, "She didn't *say* anything, and I can figure out what all that pointing and stumbling meant as well as you can." Then she glared at David and said, "Your sister, the interpreter."

David laughed. "Look, Amanda," he said,

"don't blame Janie on me. I didn't think her up."

Amanda only shrugged and went off to change her shoes; and while she was gone, another problem came up. It seemed that Marzia didn't want the twins to go along this time. "She says it's too far for them," Janie said. "She says they're too little."

"But we have to take them," David said. Dad was doing research at a library in Florence, the Thatchers were away, too, and Molly was trying to paint. "When I asked Molly if we could go, she said we could do anything we wanted as long as it was legal *and* kept the twins out of her hair today. She's working on something very important. If they can't go, we'll probably have to stay home and take care of them."

When Marzia finally understood what David was saying, she shrugged and shook her head and threw her hands in the air. He was beginning to think she was giving up on the whole expedition, when all of a sudden she nodded and said, *"Va bene,"* which can mean "okay" or "great" and things like that, but this time seemed to mean, "Okay, but don't say I didn't warn you."

"Okay, Marzia says you can go," Janie told the twins; and Esther, who had been looking very mournful, grinned and jumped up and down and said, "We're going, too, Blair. We're going too." As usual, Blair didn't say anything, but he looked at Marzia and did what Molly always called his Christmas-card-angel smile. After a minute she stopped frowning and smiled back.

When lunch was ready, Amanda went to tell Molly they were leaving, and Molly came out to say good-bye, looking the way she always did when she was painting—barefoot and paint-smeared and happy. She hugged the little kids and told everyone to be careful and to stay in the shade as much as possible because it was going to be a very hot day.

She was right about that. When they all started off up the road that led past the villa, the sun was already blazing down from almost straight overhead and there was a hot, spicy August-in-Italy smell in the air. As the road wound up the hill through the olive orchards, there were places from which you could look down to where the villa was visible—its tile roofs and thick stone walls basking in the sun, while inside the cavelike cool would last far into the day.

Farther on, not long after the olive orchards had given way to forest, they came to a place where the hill leveled out into a kind of plateau. In the midst of the level area there was a large building that looked as if it were half-barn and half-house. Chickens and turkeys scratched at the bare earth in front of the building, and off to the side there was what looked like a medium-sized used car lot. Besides several beat-up looking cars, there were two very small pickup trucks, some tractors and other farm machines, and several shiny motorcycles. Not far from the car lot a dog was chained to a doghouse made out of an old wine vat. When the dog began to bark, Marzia motioned for them all to follow her and began to run.

They went on running until they had rounded the curve in the road and were out of sight of the house. When Marzia finally let them slow down, Amanda said, "Hey, Janie. See if you can find out who lives in that house. And ask her why we were running."

Janie talked to Marzia, and then said that it was Marzia's uncle's house. "Marzia lives there too, now," Janie said. "Before her father died, she used to live in a nice house in Florence, but now she and her brothers and sisters all live there with her aunt and uncle and all their kids. She says there's too many people and she doesn't like it. And I think she said we were running because if her aunt or uncle saw her, she might have to go in and do some work instead of going on the hike." It was hard to believe that Janie had understood all that, but it seemed to make sense so nobody questioned it.

After they passed Marzia's uncle's house, they went on up the dirt road for a long, long way. They stopped once in the shade of some pine trees and ate their lunch and then went on. The sun seemed to get hotter and hotter, and the air got drier and dustier. The twins tried hard to keep up, but after a while they began to lag behind and Esther started to whine. She went on whining until Amanda yelled at her, and then she began to whimper and sniffle. So David yelled at Amanda that it wasn't Esther's fault that her legs were short and fat, and Esther yelled at David that her legs were *not* fat, and Marzia yelled something that David didn't understand but that sounded like "I told you so," and Janie yelled at everyone to shut up so she could hear what Marzia was saying. Somehow, when all the yelling was over, David was carrying Esther piggyback and thinking that he should have known enough to keep his mouth shut.

At least things were quieter after that. No one was whining or yelling, and David wasn't saying anything at all. He needed all the air he could get just to keep moving. Esther was small, but she was very solid. David's knees were beginning to wobble, and he was wondering how much longer he could keep going when Marzia stopped and pointed and said something.

"There it is," Janie translated. "That's it. That's where the dead people are."

seven

It was a church, or at least it had been one once. The crumbling walls and shattered bell tower stood at the very top of the range of hills so that, looking up, it made a dark and jagged silhouette against the sky. From where they were all standing, a steep rocky path led upwards towards the church; a path that might once have been cobblestoned, but now was only a jumble of tilted stones and deep potholes. Single file, with Marzia leading the way, they made their way over the ruts and among tentacles of thorn-covered vines to where the path ended at a gap in a tumble of stones that had once been a fence. Motioning for them to follow, Marzia climbed through the opening and into an old graveyard. Among tall weeds and more of the vicious vines, a few chipped and eroded tombstones leaned at crazy angles or lay half-buried in the weeds.

David was halfway across the graveyard, picking his way carefully among the vines and suspicious-looking mounds, when he noticed something very strange. In midstep, one foot maneuvering for a spot without thorns or dead people, he froze, listening.

What he was hearing was—dead silence. No one was talking for once, but it was more than that. The air was heavy and thick with quiet. He opened his mouth and then closed it again quickly, with an uneasy feeling that if he tried to speak the words would be soundless—smothered in the thick air. He checked the other kids, wondering if they'd noticed anything, but they were all busily picking their way through the thorns—all, that is, except Blair.

Blair was standing perfectly still. With his head turned and cocked to one side, he was obviously listening—his huge blue eyes blank and unfocused. He'd noticed all right, but even if he knew what it was that made the silence seem different, he wouldn't be able to explain it. Perhaps no one would. Perhaps it wasn't the kind of thing that could be put into words, but it seemed to have something to do with time. Centuries of time, and ancient and forgotten things.

Still poised on one foot, David teetered, regained his balance, and made his way carefully to where Blair was still standing motionless. Taking Blair's hand, he led him across the graveyard, catching up with the others just as they started through an arched doorway.

The door itself had rotted away, but a small portico still led from the graveyard into the remains of the church. The high walls still stood, but overhead there was only hot blue sky, and underfoot there was grass cluttered by fragments of ceiling beams and bits of shattered roof tile. The remains of one huge beam leaned against a wall near a crumbling altar base, and in the curved wall only empty niches showed where there must once have been gilded statues of saints and angels. Blair tugged at David's hand. "They're all gone," he said pointing at the altar wall. "Where did they all go?"

"Shh," David said. Marzia was walking towards the altar, motioning for them to follow. The bright sun beat down between the high walls, and the green grass and gray stone gleamed with heat and light, except where, just to the left of the altar, a small doorway led into darkness. Marzia was heading for the doorway.

The room beyond the altar might once have been a small chapel or sacristy. Unlike the main part of the church, the roof was still in place and the one small window was shuttered. Coming into the gloom from the bright sunlight, David felt, for a moment, blind and helpless. Something tugged at the back of his shirt, and Esther whimpered, "Hold my hand, David. I'm scared."

"Shh," David said again. In front of him he could hear Marzia whispering; and as his eyes became accustomed to the darkness, he could see that she was talking to Janie and pointing—first at the door, then at the tiny window and then down at the floor at their feet. It wasn't until then that he noticed the iron ring set in a heavy metal plate, like the covering of a manhole. Motioning for David to help her, Marzia began to tug at the ring.

The iron door was very heavy. At first it

wouldn't budge, but after trying for quite a while, they managed to lift it up out of its frame and then to slide it to one side. Below was what seemed, at first, to be total darkness. Clustering around the black hole, they all stared down into the musty-smelling nothingness and listened to what Marzia was saying. Even without knowing the words, it wasn't hard to get the drift of what she was telling —something about fear and despair and someone who called and called for help that never came. When she finally stopped talking, no one said anything for quite a long time.

"Wow," David said at last. "What did she say, Janie? Janie? JANIE." In the dim light Janie seemed to have suddenly disappeared, but she was only lying on her stomach with the whole top half of her body hanging down into the hole.

"I can see them," she said. "I think I can see them."

David grabbed her by the back of her shorts and pulled her to her feet. "Janie, you idiot. You almost fell in there. You don't know how deep it is."

"Yes I do," Janie said. "It isn't very deep. I could see the bottom. There are dead people in there. I think I saw some of them."

"Dead people?" Amanda's voice had a strangled sound. "What dead people?"

"I'm not sure," Janie said. "I didn't understand all of it, except there was something called a *rapito*, and some people got shut up down there and they died."

David remembered then that he had heard Marzia use the word *"rapito"* several times. "What's a *rapito?*" he asked.

"I don't know," Janie said. "But whatever it is, there was one, only it was a long time ago and all that's left of them is bones. I think that's what Marzia said."

"Well, I think you'd better get out of here before you get *rapito*ed, too," David said. "Go on. Get out of here. You too, twins. Amanda, help me close this door." But Amanda was leaving, too.

"Let her help you," she said. "She's the *rapito* expert."

David pulled on the ring, but by himself he couldn't begin to move it. "Marzia?" he asked, and she came over and pulled, too, and together they managed to drag it back to where it slipped into place. By the time they'd finished, his eyes were more used to the dim light, and he noticed a funny look on Marzia's face—almost as if she were trying to keep from smiling. But when they came out into the light where the others were waiting, she seemed perfectly serious again.

On the way home, except for Esther's whining and asking to be carried, no one had much to say. Perhaps it was just because they were tired; but David, at least, was doing a lot of thinking about the deserted church, the strange quiet, and the dark, musty-smelling hole under the chapel floor. Amanda, too, seemed unusually quiet and preoccupied. David remembered then that she didn't care much for spooky things, except, of course, spooky things she'd organized herself. Watching her, David got the feeling that something about the afternoon had really bothered her. And he wasn't the only one who noticed. Marzia was watching Amanda, and it occurred to David that Marzia might not be too unhappy about Amanda's being upset.

Although going downhill was easier than going up, it was still a long time before they came in sight of the plateau with the big, barny house. When they were almost there, and the house was visible through the trees, Marzia stopped suddenly, said something, and gestured down the road. Then she waved and said, *"Ciao,"* and started running through the trees towards the house.

"She said we should go on home alone," Janie said. "She said go right on down the road."

The path Marzia had taken through the trees approached the house more directly, and by the time the others reached the open area, she had disappeared, probably into the house. They went by slowly, checking out the scene again—the trucks and cars, the chickens and turkeys, the chained dog. At least David and the kids did. Amanda seemed to be still busy with whatever it was that was on her mind.

"Where did the motorciders go?" Esther asked, tugging on his shirt.

"Motorcycles, Tesser," he said. "Motor*cycles* not ciders." Feeling just generally tired and particularly tired of being tugged at, he pushed her hand away and said, "How should I know where they went?" A minute later he found out.

They heard the roar first, but the cycles were coming so fast that they barely had time to get out of the road before they swept into sight around the curve ahead. Tilting on the sharp turn, the three cyclists raced up the bumpy road toward the shed and braked to a sliding stop in a cloud of dust.

Lined up along the edge of the road, the kids stood staring after the motorcycles while the dust drifted down around them. At last Janie said, "Wowee!" She had a funny kind of open-mouthed smile on her face, and her eyes were huge and glassy looking. "Wowee!" she said again. "I'm going to do that when I get bigger."

"Not if Dad has anything to say about it, you're not," David said. "Dad says they pollute the environment and the only good thing about them is that it doesn't take them long to kill off most of the idiots who ride them." But Janie wasn't listening. Apparently forgetting all about being tired, she charged off down the road, leaning over imaginary handlebars and going, *Va—room! Va—room! Va—room!*"

Molly was starting dinner when they all trudged into the kitchen, hot and dirty and tired. She took one look at them and sent them upstairs to clean up and rest until time to eat. Janie wanted to stay and tell her all about it, but she said no.

"You run along now and rest," she told Janie. "I'll hear all about it at dinnertime. Your father will

64

be home then, and we can both hear about it at once."

Upstairs, David washed and then flaked out on his bed for a while, but he kept thinking about the church and the dark hole. He really wanted to know more about it. When he felt rested, he got up and went back downstairs. Dinner seemed to be almost ready, but Dad still wasn't back from Florence.

"Do you know if the Thatchers are home yet?" he asked Molly.

"I think so," Molly said. "I think I heard their car an hour or so ago."

David finished putting the silverware on the table, and then he said, "I think I'll run over to the Thatchers' for just a minute, okay? I want to ask them something."

"Well, don't be gone long," Molly said. "We'll be eating as soon as Jeff gets home."

David knew that besides speaking fluent Italian, the Thatchers were what Dad called Italy buffs. They were absolutely crazy about everything Italian and were real authorities about Italy in general and about Tuscany in particular. Just as he suspected, they knew all about the deserted church at the top of the ridge.

"Oh yes, we've been there several times," Olivia said. "It's a fascinating place and just far enough away for a nice comfortable hike, don't you think?"

Actually, "comfortable" wasn't exactly what he would have called it, but if you were experienced hikers like the Thatchers were, and if you weren't carrying a fat five year old, he guessed it might not be too uncomfortable. "Yeah, sure," he said. "But what I want to know is, about that hole in the floor in the little side room, like a chapel. Do you know anything about that?"

"My word," Olivia said, pulling her hands out of the bunch of clay she was pounding on and turning around to stare at David. "Andrew, did you hear that? I told you that hole was dangerous."

Andrew gave one more little tap with his hammer, leaned forward and blew the dust away, then squinted at the marble head he was working on. Finally he turned around and grinned at David. "You kiddies couldn't lift that door could you?" he asked.

David nodded. "I lifted it. Well, that is, Marzia and I lifted it together."

"You hear that?" Olivia said. "I was right. That hole should be filled up, or at least the door should be bolted down."

"Well, it is pretty heavy," David said. "Little kids couldn't lift it. But what I wanted to ask is, what is it? Why is there a hole there? Marzia was telling us something about somebody being shut up in there, but we didn't understand all of it."

"Hmm," Olivia said thoughtfully, taking another punch at the clay. "It was obviously a burial vault originally, but I did hear something else about it. I think it was Ghita who told me. Something about a feud between two old Florentine families several centuries ago. Can't remember the details, I'm afraid.

But somebody got abducted and shut up down there among the ancient bones."

"Did he die there—the person who got shut up?"

"Quite likely. Family fights were pretty serious affairs in those days."

Marzia kept saying something about a *rapito*," David said.

"*Rapito?* Oh yes, *rapire*. To kidnap. *Rapito* would be referring to a kidnapping. I imagine the victim was kidnapped for ransom, or perhaps for revenge."

"Wow," David said. The thought of being shut up in that dark hole along with a lot of dead people made his stomach do a kind of lurch. He was still just sitting there thinking about the poor guy when he heard Dad's car in the courtyard, so he thanked the Thatchers for the information and hurried home.

During dinner he waited until Amanda and Janie had told all about the hike and the church and the hole in the floor, in between arguments about who got to tell the best parts, and then he told what he'd found out from the Thatchers. Everyone was very interested—and it was kind of fun. With Janie and Amanda in the family, it wasn't too often that he got to hold the floor.

Finding out about the meaning of *rapire* led to a long conversation about kidnappings. There had been another kidnapping in the news just the day before—the son of some rich man in Milan—so kid-

67

napping was on people's minds. They discussed recent kidnappings in the States as well as in Italy, and Dad and Molly brought up some famous old kidnappings. Whenever anyone tried to change the subject, Janie brought it back to kidnapping. It was her kind of discussion, and she was obviously loving every minute of it. When everyone began to run out of kidnapping stories, she started in on the plot of some book she'd read about a girl named Isabella who got kidnapped and shut up in a tower in an old mansion. She probably would have told the whole book practically word for word if Molly hadn't convinced her she shouldn't give away the ending in case someone else might like to read it.

Okay," she said. "I won't tell the rest of it." And everyone breathed a sigh of relief. But then, just a minute later, she said, "I sure hope no one kidnaps me."

Amanda said, "Who'd want to kidnap you?"

So Janie said, "A lot of people would, that's who.".

And Amanda said, "Well, maybe. If they were running a sideshow."

And Dad yelled, "All right, that's ENOUGH!"

And that was the end of conversations about kidnapping. At least for that night.

eight

One morning in the middle of August, Amanda and David were at the Thatchers' watching Olivia modeling a Roman gladiator out of red clay and chatting about Italy in general and about people and things in and around Valle in particular. They talked first about the Bartolis, the family that had owned the villa and the land around it for generations, and then Olivia started talking about Marzia's mother.

"I admire Ghita tremendously," Olivia said. "She's had a very hard time since her husband died, and yet she's always so cheerful and positive about everything."

"What kind of hard time?" Amanda asked.

"Well, I don't think she and her children are too welcome in her sister's house, as you can imagine, but they really can't afford to live anywhere else on the money Ghita is able to earn."

"Can't her kids help out?" David asked.

Olivia shrugged. "One might think so," she said. "But from what I've heard, Marzia is the only one who helps out at all. Some of the children are still quite young, and it seems that the older boys are more inclined to add to the problem than to help out. Ghita says that whatever money they earn they spend on their cycles." Just then Olivia nodded towards the door and said, "Speaking of Marzia . . ."

Marzia was coming into the studio with Janie. Janie, as usual, was talking. She'd picked up an amazing amount of Italian, but even so, half of the words she was using were English words with Italian-sounding endings tacked on. It didn't make much sense to David, and he didn't suppose it did to Marzia either. It seemed that Janie had been trying to tell Marzia about their house in California, and the poltergeist that was supposed to have haunted it, but she had finally decided that she didn't know quite enough Italian words, so she'd come to Olivia for help.

"If I tell you about it in English, will you tell Marzia?" she asked Olivia.

"Well, my supernatural vocabulary is a bit shaky, I'm afraid," Olivia said, "but I can give it a try. I'll have to go on working while I translate, though, or this old boy is going to set before I get him into shape." So Janie told Olivia, and Olivia told Marzia, all about the ghost that was supposed to have haunted the old Westerly house and how it had thrown furniture and rocks around the house and chopped the head off the cupid on the staircase, and how, for a while after the Stanleys bought the house, it began to look as if the ghost had moved back in. As usual, Janie threw in lots of original details, and Olivia got so interested she almost forgot about fin-

70

ishing the Roman gladiator; but Marzia looked a bit skeptical, as if she thought Janie might be making the whole thing up. When Janie finished telling everything she could remember, or think of, about the Westerly House, she asked Marzia if there were any haunted houses around Valle.

Olivia translated the question, and Marzia shook her head.

"Or ghosts?" Janie asked. "Or witches?"

"Le streghe?" Olivia asked Marzia.

"No," Marzia said, but then she said, *"Oh, sì. C'e uno stregone."*

"Marzia says there is a male witch," Olivia said. "I think I've heard of the one she's referring to. He was pointed out to me once in the village. Actually I think he's more what we might call a witch doctor, or even a faith healer. I think he may predict the future a bit and things of that sort, but mostly people take their health problems to him. Last spring Ghita told me about taking one of her younger children to him with some kind of digestive problem, if I remember correctly. Anyway, whatever the problem was, the witch doctor told her what to do and she did it and the child recovered very quickly."

Up to that point Amanda had been looking rather bored; but when Olivia started telling about the witch doctor, she suddenly began to listen very carefully. When she asked Olivia to explain some more about exactly what a witch doctor did, David wasn't surprised, because when Dad and Molly were first married, Amanda had been studying to be a witch. She'd been into learning about making spells and potions and philters and doing seances and all kinds of things like that. But then, when it began to look as if the real, original poltergeist had moved back into the Westerly House, Amanda had suddenly seemed to lose interest in the supernatural. Lately she'd been more into records and rock stars and people of the opposite sex. It had been quite a while since David had heard her mention anything about spells or potions or even curses, which had been sort of her specialty. But now it was obvious that she was very interested in the Italian witch doctor.

"Does he do curses and love philters and things like that?" she asked Olivia, but when Olivia started to translate the question into Italian, Amanda stopped her. "Never mind asking her," she said. "I just wondered if you knew."

David began to get the picture. He grinned, thinking maybe he ought to warn poor old Hilary if Amanda was thinking of going shopping for a love philter. Olivia was leaning over the gladiator at the moment, so she didn't see Amanda kick David in the shins. Actually David didn't see the kick himself, but he certainly felt it. "Wow," he said, moving out of range. "What was that for?" But he knew, really. It was for the grin, and for guessing what Amanda was up to. He knew what she was up to, and she knew he knew. Not that that was going to stop her, he thought, and he was right. It didn't. Before they left the Thatchers' that day, a visit to the witch doctor was all arranged.

It turned out to be another long walk, at least as far as the abandoned church. But it wasn't as steep a road, and fortunately it turned out to be a much cooler day. This time the little kids kept up without so much trouble. David had talked to Esther about how he was tired of carrying people, and if she wanted to come along she'd have to do it on her own feet and without whining. Since she didn't want to be left behind, she promised, and on the whole trip she only whined softly a few times; and when David reminded her of her promise, she stopped.

Actually, although the whole trip had been Amanda's idea, she was the only one who caused any problems on the way there. This time she'd insisted on wearing her sandals, and even when Marzia said she should change them, she refused. So all the way there, she kept getting pebbles in her shoes and having to stop and shake them out; and then when they were almost there, she stepped in a rut and turned her ankle. She sat down on the road for a while, moaning and saying that her ankle was probably broken or at least sprained. But it didn't seem to be swelling, and after a while she managed to go on, with a very bad limp.

The witch doctor lived on the other side of the Valle di Chiesa, so the trip had consisted of going down the hill to the village, through it, and then up a long narrow valley in the other direction. It was an interesting walk, but all the way David kept wondering if there was any point in actually trying to see the witch doctor. It seemed to him that it was likely the witch doctor didn't give interviews to a bunch of kids; and even if he did, he might charge more than the three thousand lire they're managed to scrape up between them, which after all, was only a little more than three dollars.

When they finally got to the witch doctor's house, David was really surprised. He didn't know exactly what he'd been expecting, but he guessed it must have been something spooky, like a tumbledown shack in a dark forest, or maybe even a cave. So when it turned out that the witch doctor lived in a modern-looking brick and plaster house on what seemed to be a very prosperous farm, he felt a little disappointed, at least at first.

They walked up the long driveway toward the house, past an enclosure where huge shaggy cattle with long horns were grazing, and then between pens of sheep and pigs. Beyond the house there were several barns and sheds, and on one side there was a large parking lot. There were four cars in the parking lot. But just as they were arriving, a group of people came out of the house and got into one of the cars and drove away. So it looked as if there weren't too many customers ahead of them. They all sat down on a wall to wait and watch what was going on.

A man and woman and little boy who had been standing in front of the house went in, and two old ladies got out of their car and went to wait their turn by the front door. The only other person who seemed to be in line was a man who was leaning against a funny little three wheeled pickup truck. He was a big man with bulgy muscles and red cheeks, and he certainly didn't look as if he had anything wrong with him.

"I wonder what he's going to ask the witch doctor," David said. "He doesn't look sick to me."

"What are we going to ask about?" Janie said. "None of us is sick, either."

"I think we ought to go in one at a time," Amanda said. "Then each of us can ask him whatever we want to."

"Did you have something in particular that you wanted to ask about?" David asked, being careful to keep a straight face—and his shins out of reach, just in case.

Amanda glared at him. "Maybe," she said.

"But what if he doesn't speak English?" Janie said, and for a minute David felt shocked—at himself for not having thought of that possibility. Amanda went around all the time expecting everybody to speak English, but he hadn't thought that he did.

"Well, of course he speaks English," Amanda said. "Olivia said he was a famous witch doctor and people even come from other countries to see him. He'd have to speak English."

David shook his head. "You know something," he said, "Janie is probably right. Ask Marzia, Janie."

So Janie asked Marzia, and she didn't seem to know either. She thought for a while, and then she went over to where the man was leaning against the truck. When she came back, she said the man didn't know if the doctor spoke English, but he didn't think so.

"Marzia says that man is a farmer," Janie said, "and he's come to see the doctor about his sick cows. And he told Marzia that if we're going to ask about a person, we have to have something with us that belongs to the person, like a shirt or handkerchief or a piece of jewelry."

"Well, that settles that," David said. "He hadn't been too crazy about talking to the witch doctor anyway, and since they hadn't brought anything that belonged to a sick person, there wouldn't be any point in trying. But then Marzia pointed to the ring on Amanda's finger and motioned for her to take it off. When she got the ring, Marzia held it up and talked for quite a while to Janie.

"Marzia says we're going to ask the witch doctor about Amanda," Janie said. "She says we're going to ask for a *predizione* for Amanda."

"*Predizione?*" Amanda said. "What does that mean? Is that like a prediction, of the future?" She looked at Marzia suspiciously for a minute. "A prediction of my future?" But then she shrugged. "Okay," she said. "Why not."

The witch doctor turned out to be almost as unspooky as his house. He was a small man with short gray hair and a normal-looking middle-aged face. The only things that made him at all unusual were his clothing and his eyes. He was wearing a long black robe with a high collar, almost like a priest's outfit, and his eyes were small and dark and very bright. When he looked at you, you felt that he was seeing more than most people did. When they all filed in to his little room, he looked hard at each one of them, and they were all very quiet. When the dark, bright eyes looked at him, David felt certain they could see that he'd only come on a kind of adventure. But the witch doctor didn't sound angry when he talked to Marzia. He took the ring and held it in the palm of his hand for a while. Then he went behind a little desk and sat down. On the desk there were three shallow bowls of what seemed to be ordinary water. The witch doctor took a little bottle out of a drawer and poured a few drops of something that looked like olive oil in each of the bowls. The oil separated into little blobs and moved around on top of the water, and when it stopped moving, the witch doctor looked at it very carefully for quite a long time. Then he talked to Marzia, except that some of the time he seemed to be talking to Janie, and then he got up and went to the door and held it open for them to go out. Marzia gave him the three thousand lire, and he smiled and gave it back and went back into his office and closed the door.

Of course, Amanda was very impatient to hear what the witch doctor had said about her; and as soon as they were all out in the parking lot again, she started saying, "What did he say, Janie? What did he say?"

But Janie had to confer with Marzia for a long time before she began to translate. Finally she said,

"Okay, everybody. I'm ready. The first thing the witch doctor said was about Amanda's foot. And I understood most of it when he said it, before Marzia told me. He said the person whose ring it was had hurt her foot—"

"See!" Amanda said to David. "I told you it was really sprained."

"—but that it wasn't very bad and that it would be all right soon," Janie went on. "But *then*—he started talking about *pericolo*. He said that the person whose ring it was, was in '*molto pericolo*' and that she'd better be very careful."

"What's *pericolo?*" Esther said, tugging at David. "What's *pericolo?*"

Now that Janie mentioned it, David suddenly remembered hearing the witch doctor say that particular word several times, but it wasn't until now that he realized he knew what it meant, too. "It means—" His voice came out funny, and he found he had to stop and swallow. "It means danger," he told Esther. Esther began to whimper.

"Is that all he said?" Amanda asked. "Didn't he say what the danger was?"

"Nooo," Janie said thoughtfully. "Just that you'd better be careful."

Marzia grabbed Janie's arm and pulled her a few steps away and talked to her for quite a while. From her tone of voice, it sounded as if she didn't think Janie had told it right. David didn't get much of what she was saying except for the word "*padre*." It seemed as if Marzia was saying something about

Amanda's father. Janie was listening very carefully, but she seemed puzzled or maybe doubtful. Finally she said, "Marzia says the witch doctor said that Amanda ought to go away because of the danger. She says that the witch doctor said Amanda ought to go back to live with her rich father in California."

"Back to California?" David asked.

"That's what Marzia says," Janie said; but David got the feeling that Janie wasn't too sure she'd gotten it right.

"The witch doctor said I ought to go back to California?" Amanda asked.

"Marzia says he did," Janie said.

Amanda gave Marzia one of her long, cool looks. "Yeah," she said at last. "I'll bet she did."

On the way home David had lots of time to think about the witch doctor's prediction. It was obvious that Amanda thought Marzia had made up the part about going back to California; and when he thought about it, David had to admit he hadn't noticed the witch doctor saying the word "California," which was a word he would surely have recognized. On the other hand, however, he *had* heard the *pericolo* himself. There wasn't much doubt that the witch doctor had said that Amanda was in some sort of danger. All the way home, and for quite a while afterward, he wondered what kind of danger it might be; but then, with things like Venice and Verona and the beginning of school to think about, it slowly got crowded out of his mind.

nine

Right at the end of the summer, the Stanleys decided to go on one last sightseeing trip before school started —this time to Venice and Verona. They were all mad about Venice. Riding in water taxis and gondolas, watching the glass blowers, getting lost in the maze of tiny streets and squares and feeding the pigeons in front of San Marco's appealed to everyone; and the whole time they were there, Molly was in such a haze of excitement about form and light and color that she had to be watched to keep her from walking into walls and off bridges.

Verona was great, too, particularly Romeo's and Juliet's houses. Dad brought along a copy of the play, and in the hotel room, the night before, he told the story and read the parts that weren't too hard for the little kids to understand. He did a great job of it, and everybody got into the story. So when they actually got there and went through the rooms and stood on Juliet's balcony, it made a big impression on all of them. Particularly on Janie, who went around being Juliet for days afterwards. Even after they got back home to the villa, Janie kept hanging out of windows and yelling, "Wherefore art thou, Romeo?" and stabbing herself with imaginary daggers and dying dramatically all over everywhere; until Dad got tired of it and told her that from then on she could only commit suicide in her own bedroom, and quietly.

Even without the trip, every day would have been busy. Along with hikes and picnics and explorations—and for Dad and Molly, painting and research and writing—everyone was gradually learning how to cope with the Italian way of life. Like learning how to count out the thousands of lire it takes to buy anything, how to eat spaghetti properly, and where to find the things they needed to buy—like matches, which are only sold at the tobacconist. Dad, in particular, learned how to collect belongings sent to Italy by ship—a procedure that used up time and money and patience, not to mention a huge stack of form letters and an awful lot of rubber stamp ink. Dad said that if he were Italian, he'd certainly try to corner the rubber stamp business and become the world's richest man.

Being so busy made the time go very fast, and all of a sudden it was almost time for school to start, and nothing had been done about finding out where everyone would be going. The twins were no problem. They had just barely turned five, and Blair, at least, was young for his age in some ways. So it was decided that they would just stay home for one more year. Janie could go to the village school. Her Italian was already very good, and she didn't seem to be at all nervous about going to school in a new language. The real problem concerned David and Amanda. From what they'd been able to find out, the local school was quite different from an American junior high school, in more ways than just the difference in language. Of course, Marzia went there, which to David was a plus; nevertheless whenever he thought about it, it made him nervous. As for Amanda, she said she wasn't going to go. David had never had much luck telling Dad he wasn't going to do something when Dad said he was, but he was considering giving it one more try when another possibility came up.

At the university where she was taking a painting class, someone told Molly about a school in Florence where all the teachers were from America and the instruction was in English. So she stopped by the school on her way home from Florence and the information she got was really interesting. The school was in a beautiful old palace on a hill across the Arno River from Florence; the classes were small; there was instruction in all the arts; and the students got to go on excursions to famous places, not only in Florence, but also in other nearby cities like Siena and Pisa. Most of the students were from American families who happened to be living in Florence, but there were quite a few from other places all over the world. Molly thought that David and Amanda would love it. It would be expensive, she said; but with the inheritance, they would be able to afford it. Dad thought it was a fantastic opportunity, and David thought it sounded okay. Amanda didn't think she was going to like it until she heard that the Morehouses had enrolled Hilary there, too. After that she couldn't wait for school to start.

Leaving out the ordinary things that make going to school very interesting at times and a pain in the neck at others, the school in Florence turned out to be great in some highly unusual ways. One of the ways was the building itself. It had been a castle originally, with a moat and fortified walls, but the castle had been mostly destroyed by invaders and rebuilt as a grand Renaissance palace. For kids who were used to the chicken-coop contemporary of most modern American school buildings, it was mind-blowing just to find yourself attending classes in rooms with enormous fireplaces, ancient hand-carved wood paneling, and ceilings that were beamed and crossbeamed or painted by Renaissance artists.

For the first couple of weeks David couldn't get used to it. He'd look up in the middle of a math problem or a grammar lesson and look around, and all of a sudden he'd feel as if he could almost tune in on all the secrets of the palace's past—as if he were moving through time, and any moment he might become aware of some strange event that the old walls had witnessed hundreds of years before. Once he got the same feeling in the midst of a soccer game—a game played on a wide terrace with a high palace wall on one sideline, and an incredible view of the whole city of Florence on the other. The feeling of moving through time started during a time out, but he was still in the past, staring down the hill at the lances and banners of an invading army when the game got underway again. He didn't come back to the present until a soccer ball bounced off the side of his head.

Another good thing about the school was the fact that it was an easy place to get acquainted. Since almost everyone was from a family that was only temporarily in Florence, there weren't any of the usual tight little groups that had been best friends for years and didn't want or need anyone new. Within a very few days, David had met almost everybody and had made a couple of special friends—a guy from Israel and another one who was half-Italian and half-American.

As far as learning went, the school was pretty much like most schools—what people learned depended on what they wanted to learn. But there was one thing the school did an especially good job of teaching: Italy. Not long after school started, David noticed that he was really seeing things he'd only looked at before—buildings, works of art, even people. Something—maybe it was partly the palace itself —was doing a good job of teaching Italy appreciation. Not long after he realized that he was seeing a lot of things differently, he heard Amanda, who had always made a point of either yawning or giggling at Italian art, having a violent argument about whether Donatello or Cellini was the best sculptor. So then he knew it probably worked on everybody.

After a while Amanda even admitted that she

liked the school, too. Like David, she got to know everyone in a hurry, and everyone got to know her even faster. She even went so far as to say a couple of her teachers were okay, which was, for Amanda, almost unheard-of. But what she liked most of all was the ride back and forth to school every day. The Stanleys and the Morehouses were taking turns driving Hilary and Amanda and David to school, so twice a day Amanda was sharing a back seat with Old Knobby Knees, and she couldn't have been happier, even though he usually read a book or did math problems and never paid any attention to her at all.

As far as David was concerned, being in love made Amanda harder to get along with in some ways, and a little easier in others. On the one hand, she started getting up in the morning without having to be called half a dozen times—but she also started shutting herself in the bathroom for hours to fool with her face and hair, so nobody else could get in, even in an emergency. And because Hilary was such a math nut, she started getting *A*'s and *B*'s in math, after having flunked it on principle most of her life. But as far as her temper went, it was mostly just more unpredictable. One minute she would be so sweet and friendly you'd hardly know her, and the next she'd bite someone's head off for practically no reason at all.

The only reason David sometimes felt sorry that they were going to the American school was because of Marzia. After school started, Marzia didn't come to the villa so often, and when she did come, she didn't spend any time with the Stanleys. David wasn't sure why. It might have been because she was angry at David and Amanda for deciding not to go to her school; but if that was it, it probably was only part of it. David felt sure the main reason she was staying away was that Amanda and Hilary were spending so much time together on the way to school every day. Marzia probably thought Hilary was definitely Amanda's boyfriend now, and there wasn't any use for her to try to get his attention anymore.

If that was it, and David was pretty sure it was, it was too bad someone didn't set her straight. But he knew better than to tell Janie to tell Marzia that Hilary still hadn't even gotten around to noticing that Amanda had a crush on him—because if he did, Janie would be sure to tell Amanda that he'd said so, and Amanda would be furious. And they'd been in the same family long enough for him to have learned that you didn't go around making Amanda furious on purpose, unless of course you really wanted to die young or something. So until he learned enough Italian to tell Marzia himself, she was just going to have to go on thinking that Hilary and Amanda were doing a Romeo and Juliet every day in the back seat of the car.

So that was the way things were for several weeks. Dad did research at the university, Molly painted, the twins played around the villa, Janie went to school in the village and came back speaking more Italian every day and knowing the names and ages and life histories of nearly everyone in the village,

and David and Amanda were having what Dad called
a once-in-a-lifetime educational experience in Florence. And then, in the middle of October, Dad and
Molly decided to spend a few days in Rome.

ten

The trip to Rome was a birthday present for Molly, and it was because of Olivia Thatcher that Dad and Molly went alone. The idea got started one evening when Molly was talking about how she was dying to see the Sistine Chapel, and Olivia offered to baby-sit so Dad could take Molly on a kidless trip to Rome as a birthday present. They were all sitting around the fire in the huge living room in the Stanleys' part of the villa. When Olivia made the suggestion, Molly pretended to faint. Then she jumped up and ran around to Olivia and hugged her and kissed her on both cheeks and said, "The poor woman's out of her mind, but don't think I'm not going to take advantage of her. When can we leave, Jeff?"

Everyone laughed, and Olivia said she was serious and it wouldn't be any trouble at all and she'd really enjoy it. She loved having the twins around, and everyone else would be away at school most of the time.

"How do you feel about this offer?" Dad asked Andrew, and Andrew said it was fine with him.

"I'll run over and ask the Morehouses if they

can drive every day next week," Amanda said. As she ran out of the room, all the adults raised their eyebrows and grinned about Amanda's crush on Hilary.

So it was all arranged. Because the Thatchers actually lived in the same building, the Stanley kids could all sleep in their own rooms at night, and David and Amanda would be responsible for everything in the morning, making breakfast and getting themselves and Janie off to school. But in the evening they would all have dinner with the Thatchers, and Olivia and Andrew would be in charge of settling arguments and giving permission for any out-of-the-ordinary projects. "Such as the adoption of stray polar bears and whether or not to build a spaceship in the living room," Dad said.

"I think Livy and I could handle that lot," Andrew said, "but on the close ones, we're apt to get a hung jury."

"In that case," Dad said, "say no. With this bunch *no* is usually the safest answer." But that was just kidding, Dad told David and Amanda later. "Actually," Dad said on Monday morning when he and Molly were getting ready to leave, "I have a great deal of faith in your ability to take care of yourselves and the little kids and to look after things around the house while we're gone."

Although Dad and Molly left early in the morning, Janie and the twins woke up in time to see them off. Molly hugged everyone two or three times each and told Janie to eat enough and not be fussy about what she ate, and Esther not to eat too much, and everybody to be careful and do exactly what Andrew and Olivia told them to. Then the kids all ran out to the terrace wall to watch and wave as the car passed below them and wound its way down the dirt road toward the village and beyond it to the autostrada that led to Rome.

Perhaps it was just the novelty of being on their own, but everything went surprisingly well that morning. David and Amanda made an extra big breakfast, cleaned up the kitchen, and got Janie off to school and the twins next door to the Thatchers' without a single argument. And that evening at the Thatchers' things continued to go well. Everyone was on his and her best behavior at dinner. Janie ate what was put on her plate, and Esther, who wasn't supposed to ask for seconds, didn't. Afterwards David and Amanda helped Andrew clean up the kitchen, because Olivia had done the cooking, and then they all sat around in the studio and talked until it was time for the twins to go to bed.

Back in their own part of the villa, David and Amanda flipped a coin to see who would take the first turn putting the twins to bed—and David lost. He wondered afterwards if everything would have turned out differently if he had won. But the way it did happen was that David said, "Heads," and the coin came down tails, so he went up and helped the twins with their baths. When he came back downstairs about twenty minutes later, he could tell right away that something out of the ordinary had happened. Janie was waiting for him in the door of the living room.

"Amanda got a letter," she said as soon as David was in the room. Amanda was on her knees arranging some logs in the fireplace, but she didn't turn around or say anything.

"A letter?" David asked. "When?"

"Just now," Janie said. "Just a few minutes ago. Somebody knocked on the door, and I got there first and there wasn't anybody there, except there was a letter lying right there in front of the door and it said Amanda on it."

Amanda muttered something about a blabbermouth and went on fooling with the fire.

"Who was it from?" David asked her.

She stood up finally, dusting off her hands, and leaned against the mantel watching the fire. Her face was still turned away. "Not that it's anyone's business," she said. "But it happened to be from Hilary."

"From Hilary?"

"Yes from *Hilary*," Amanda said, and it was obvious that she was angry. David couldn't think why—until it suddenly dawned on him that it was because he had sounded so surprised.

Still too surprised to start using his head he asked, "What did he say?" The moment he said it, he knew he'd made another mistake. If she wanted him to know she'd tell him and if she didn't she wouldn't, and asking her was the best way to make sure she didn't.

"That," Amanda said, "is my business."

David nodded. It figured. It was cold in the living room, and it was going to take a long time before the fire that Amanda had built would start making a difference. "Why are you lighting a fire now?" he asked. "It's almost time to go to bed."

"I have some homework to do," Amanda said. "And I want to do it down here. Any more questions?"

"You don't need to be sarcastic," David said. "It just seemed like a waste of wood to start one so late." The heater in Amanda's small bedroom would have heated it up in a few minutes. He shrugged and walked to the long narrow windows that looked out over the front terrace. By cupping his hands to shut out the light from the room, he could see into the night.

The night looked cold, too. The October weather had been perfect lately, warm and clear, but now suddenly there was a faint hint of winter in the air. Beyond the window a nearly full moon was turning the terrace into a sleek, silvery meadow, tiger-striped by the long thin shadows of the cypresses. Everything was cold and still and mysteriously lifeless.

Up until that moment, to be left more or less on their own for five days had seemed fun and exciting. But now, suddenly, David wished Dad and Molly were back. Behind him, Amanda's fire had begun to flare up, and its reflection flickered in the window like a witch's fire at the edge of the forest.

Where he stood, near the windows, it was still cold and damp. He shivered.

"I'm going up and read in bed," he said. "You'd better go to bed, too, Janie."

"I still have half an hour," Janie said. "Can I stay down here with you, Amanda?"

Amanda shrugged. "If you keep your mouth shut," she said. "And I mean *shut*."

Janie stared at Amanda for a minute and then, obviously deciding it wouldn't be worth the effort, she sighed and followed David upstairs.

In bed with a book, David thought for a while about Amanda and the letter before he started to read. He couldn't imagine why Hilary would have written to her. He considered the possibility that it had something to do with the ride to school in the morning. The Morehouses were supposed to be driving, and maybe something had gone wrong with their car? But, in that case, why didn't he just knock and come in and say so. As for its being a love note or something like that—it just didn't seem possible. After all, David rode to Florence and back every day with Amanda and Hilary and if Hilary was the least bit interested in Amanda, he certainly deserved an Oscar for the way he was acting as if he didn't know she existed.

He gave up trying to figure it out and started to read, but the book wasn't too interesting and his eyes were beginning to feel heavy. The next thing he knew it must have been at least an hour later and he was being awakened by having his head banged against the headboard of the bed. He'd fallen asleep still propped up in a sitting position, and now Janie was kneeling beside him, shaking him to so hard that his head was jerking back and forth, and her fingernails were digging into his shoulders. The first thing he felt was angry.

"Stop it, Janie," he said. "You're scratching me. What's the matter?"

"It's Amanda," Janie said. "I think she's eloping with Hilary."

David was still a little angry about being scratched or he probably would have laughed. As it was, he just put his hand over his eyes and sighed. "Janie," he said at last, "you are out of your so-called mind. Amanda and Hilary are not eloping. What makes you think they're eloping?"

"Because," Janie said. She was teetering on her knees on the edge of the bed, and her eyes were absolutely enormous with excitement. She was dressed in her pajamas and bathrobe so she'd had time to get ready for bed before—before whatever it was that had given her such a crazy idea had occurred. David wondered briefly if she might have been asleep and dreamed it.

"Because," Janie said again, "I was talking to the twins a few minutes ago—" She paused, glancing at David sideways. She wasn't supposed to keep the twins awake past their bedtime. "—because they couldn't sleep." (I'll bet they couldn't, David thought. Not with Janie talking to them, they couldn't.) "—

94

and I heard something, and I snuck out and Amanda was going down the stairs with her coat on and everything. So I followed her, and she went downstairs and out the front door and across the terrace towards the stairs to the *passeggiata*."

Suddenly David was wide awake. Of course Janie was wrong about Amanda and Hilary eloping, but what on earth *was* she up to, sneaking out of the house at this hour of the night? He got out of bed, pulled on his pants over his pajama bottoms, and got into his shoes and bathrobe, while Janie circled around him, tiptoeing with excitement and jabbering away like an excited chipmunk about Amanda and Hilary and eloping and Romeo and Juliet and all kinds of nonsense. When he was dressed and starting down the stairs, she ran after him calling, "What are you going to do? What are you going to do, David?"

He realized then that he hadn't the slightest idea. "I don't know," he said. "I'm just going to look around a little. You go back to bed, and I'll come and tell you about it in a few minutes. Okay?"

When Janie started arguing that she wanted to go along and David said she couldn't, she gave up so quickly that he should have been suspicious. He probably would have been if he hadn't had his mind so much on other things. As soon as he was out of the door, he started running; he was halfway across the first grape vine terrace when an idea occurred to him, and he turned back towards *Il Fienile*.

Mrs. Morehouse was always talking about how Hilary did homework and math problems until eleven o'clock every night—so he should be at his desk right now—unless, of course, Janie was right, which David didn't believe for a minute. He'd been in Hilary's room and remembered that his desk sat right by the window—so it should be easy to tell if he were still there or not. Sure enough, as soon as David rounded the corner of the house, he could see that the desk lamp was on in Hilary's room, but he couldn't quite see the level at which a head, bent over a math book, would be. But if he went back a little way. . . . A moment later he had run back across the courtyard, climbed up on the wall—and there he was. Old Knobby Knees was just where his mother said he always was, scrunched down over some fascinating math problem.

David was climbing down off the wall, feeling rather pleased with himself—just call me David Sherlock Stanley—when it suddenly hit him that the case wasn't exactly solved yet. The big mystery, in fact, was still as mysterious as ever: where was Amanda, and why? And, if Hilary hadn't written the letter that had been left on the front step—which certainly had something to do with Amanda's disappearance—who had? It was right then, standing there by the wall in the cold moonlight, that he began to look at the whole thing very differently, and to see how bad it really looked. And then to make matters worse, a couple of words popped into his head as if out of nowhere. The words were *"molto pericolo."* The witch doctor had said that Amanda was in *molto pericolo.* A prickling shiver ran up his spine and into the back of his head. A minute later he was running again, back around the house and across the moonlit terrace in the direction of the *passeggiata*.

It was dark on the path under the trees, and the ruts and tree roots made it impossible to run without tripping. Stopping every few yards to listen, he hurried along the path as fast as he dared, slipping and stumbling on the uneven surface. The first urn scared him half to death, materializing from black nothingness into a ghostly white shape with startling suddenness. Warning himself to be ready for the second one, he stumbled on for such a long time that he began to think he'd somehow missed it, before it finally appeared—a vague blur of light that gradually firmed into an urn and pedestal. He was only a few steps past the second urn when fear exploded, jolting him off his feet and jangling out to the ends of his fingers and toes. Somebody had screamed. He'd already turned to run back the way he'd come when he realized that the scream was familiar.

Somehow, without actually deciding to do it, he found himself turning again and running—toward where something terrible was happening to Amanda. He was still running when he reached the picnic terrace. Moonlight was flooding into the circular area around the stone table. He could clearly see the table —the benches, the water trough, but nothing else. No one was there—but someone was not far away. It sounded as if a lot of people were just beyond the clearing, trampling around in the underbrush on the steep slope that led down to the road. He could hear

97

feet thudding, brush crackling, and voices muttering unintelligibly. Standing near the table, his heart thundering against his ribs, he tried to think what to do. The struggle was gradually moving down the slope, and no one seemed aware of his presence. He could still have turned and run and perhaps have gotten away—but then Amanda screamed again, and without stopping to think of the consequences, he started to yell.

"Stop! Help! Help, police!" he shouted. He was still shouting when someone charged back up the slope and into the clearing. David let out one last yell and began to run. He ran around the stone table, missed the entrance to the path in the dim light, and started around again. Heavy footsteps pounded close behind him, and out of the corner of his eye he glimpsed a dark, shadowy figure. Realizing that he was the faster on the tight turns around the table, he kept circling, afraid to break for the path. They'd circled several times when the noisy clomping stopped suddenly—and David braked and turned back, barely in time to avoid running right into his pursuer's arms.

For a moment then they faced each other across the table, and for the first time David really saw him —a man with no head. In the tiniest fraction of a second, a whole stream of ideas ran through his mind. "This can't be real—no one runs around without a head—it must be a nightmare—just a nightmare, and in a moment I'll wake up." But then the figure moved slightly, the light changed, and David saw that instead of being headless, the man was hooded. His head was covered by a tight-fitting black hood, which had been invisible in the darkness. But now the head was visible—a dark oval, blank and faceless except for two eyeholes looking, in the dim light, like enormous round eyes.

The man leaned on the table breathing heavily, and then suddenly feinted to the left. David ran too, saw the ruse, and again managed to change direction in time to keep from being caught. They were running again, to the right, when David became aware of a high-pitched squealing noise and something shot out of the bushes directly into his path. He swerved to miss it, stumbled, and the hooded man caught up with him, ran into him, and they both fell.

The man came down on top of David, pinning him to the ground, just as the small squealing thing came back into David's line of vision. It was Janie, and she was swinging a big stick. There was a swish and a thud and the man on David's back made a yelping noise and lunged at Janie. Scrambling to his feet, David yelled, "Run, Janie. Run for help."

She backed away swinging the stick with both hands, but then as she turned to run, the hooded man grabbed her from behind, lifting her off her feet. But she went right on screaming and flailing away with the heavy stick, and kicking now, too, with both feet. Trying to get to her to pull her free, David was suddenly aware of another person, jumping around beside him. Another hooded man was trying to get to Janie—lunging and ducking and grabbing at her

99

stick. But then he noticed David and grabbed him instead. David struggled, but the other guy was a lot stronger. Very quickly he had David pinned, holding him from behind with his arm across his throat. They'd gotten the stick away from Janie, and the man who was holding her had his hand across her mouth. Suddenly everything was very quiet except for a mumbling, smothered sound from Janie.

There were three of them now. The third man, hooded too, looked enormous. He gestured toward the path to the road and whispered in Italian. He sounded angry and urgent, and immediately they started across the terrace, pushing David and carrying Janie with them. They were starting down the steep path that led to the quarry road when one of the men spoke sharply, and they all stopped and listened.

Something was moving in the underbrush on the other side of the circle. There was a sound like footsteps and rustling leaves. The third man started back stealthily like a stalking cat, creeping toward the sounds in the underbrush. He was near the table when the man who was holding Janie gasped and jerked his hand away from her mouth and shook it.

Janie yelled, "Run, twins. Run for help." And the next moment everything went crazy. The clearing around the picnic table seemed to be full of people running in every direction—stumbling, falling, and getting up and running again. The man who was holding David made a grab at someone who was running past, and David jerked away and ran too, until something tripped him and he fell and his head hit something very hard. Lights flared up around him, and then everything went black.

eleven

He didn't stay unconscious for very long. They were still carrying him, slipping and jolting on the steep hill, when he began to be aware of what was happening. His head was hurting like crazy, and at first he couldn't remember anything except that he knew something was very wrong and he was frightened. Then the jolting stopped, and he felt himself being lifted up and put down on a cold, hard surface. There was a loud metallic clang, followed by darkness and what sounded like a lot of people crying softly. A moment later a motor started, and the hard surface under his back began to vibrate. He tried to push himself to a sitting position and moaned as a pain shot through his head.

"David," Amanda's voice came out of the pitch darkness. "David, are you all right?" Amanda's voice sounded tense and shaky, but she didn't seem to be crying.

"I don't know," he said, but it came out sounding like a groan. The crying got louder and more frantic, and he added quickly, "I'm okay, I think. I must have been knocked out, but I'm okay now."

The metal floor lurched and jolted, and David was tipped back against a wall. He moaned again, and Amanda said, "Where does it hurt?" He felt her hand on his arm and he took it and guided it to the place where his head felt as if it were about to come apart.

"Be careful," he said. He had wanted to touch it himself and had been afraid to. "Not so hard. It hurts."

He winced at Amanda's exploring fingers, but when she said, "I don't think it's bleeding. There's a lump but I don't feel any blood," he started feeling a little better, because what he'd been imagining was a big bloody hole. He steadied himself against the wall behind him and started feeling around him for the kids. They were all there, a jumble of arms and legs and tear-wet faces. "Janie?" he said. "Blair? Tesser?" and they answered by grabbing hold of him and crying louder than ever.

It was becoming obvious that they were in the back of a small truck. The growling motor whined through a series of gear shifts and the metal floor beneath them tipped and jolted. The little kids were clutching David, hanging onto his bathrobe, pulling him this way and that as the truck bounced and lurched. His head was still throbbing, and then the top of someone's head hit his chin as the truck tilted, making him bite his tongue. All three of the little kids were crying as steadily and monotonously as a broken record, and for quite a long time David was so close to crying himself he didn't dare try to say anything.

All he could do was clench his teeth and swallow hard and pat whichever kid seemed to be crying hardest. Most of the time it was Esther, but sometimes it was Blair, and once it was even Janie. It really scared him when it was Janie—probably because he couldn't remember another time in Janie's whole lifetime when she'd cried because she was frightened—angry maybe, or sad, or even just for the fun of it, but never before because she was frightened.

So he just clenched his teeth and patted and tried to put things together in his head in a way that made some sense. His thoughts seemed to be coming in a jumble of bits and pieces, and mixed up with everything he tried to think through were a few Italian words that kept scaring him half to death. The words were *"molto pericolo"* and *"rapito."* One minute he would be hearing the witch doctor's voice saying, *"molto pericolo,"* and the next there'd be Olivia saying, *"Rapito—rapito* would mean a kidnapping." And then there were other bits of things that Olivia had said—phrases like "kidnapped for ransome" and "shut up down there among the ancient bones."

Sometime later he noticed that the truck was running more smoothly, as if it were on a paved highway, and it occurred to him that he ought to be listening for sounds and counting turns and all the things that kidnapped people did in stories so they could tell where they were being taken. So he tried a little, but he was too jittery to keep his mind on it for very long. He did notice that the road got bumpy and then smooth again several times, and that they kept on traveling for what seemed like hours and hours. The pain in his head had faded to a dull ache and his body had begun to ache almost as much from bouncing on the metal truck bed when there was a sudden sharp turn that slid them all together in a heap. For a minute or two they seemed to be climbing steeply up a very rough road, and then the truck ground and shivered to a stop. Everybody clutched each other and waited.

There was the sound of the cab doors opening and then slamming shut, and then footsteps and voices that came around toward the back of the truck. The kids had stopped crying, but David could hear their hearts pounding, or else, maybe, it was his own. There was a grating sound at the back of the truck, a squeak of hinges, and then someone—it could have been David himself—gave a sharp gasp.

Moonlight flooded through the dome-shaped opening, silhouetting three terrible figures, black and blank and featureless, except where the eyeholes in the dark hoods gave the impression of enormous owl-like eyes. They just stood there, peering into the back of the truck for what seemed like a very long time, and after a while Esther began to cry again—a thin, high-pitched wailing noise. When Esther wailed, one of the black figures stepped back and turned to look at the one in the middle. The man in the middle seemed to be in charge, because as Esther went on wailing the other two guys went on looking at him, as if for instructions. After a while he said, *"Venite qui,"* in a deep, gruff voice.

Janie jerked David's arm. "He said come here," she whispered and David whispered back, "I know," but he didn't move and neither did anyone else. Then the tall kidnapper in the middle said something else, and the other two shook their heads. Very suddenly the big guy jumped up into the back of the truck and started groping his way toward where they were all huddled together. As he got close, one of the little kids screamed and then the groping hands touched David and pulled him to his feet.

As the kidnapper jerked David towards the tail-gate, the other two reached up and pulled him down to the ground. He had time for a brief glimpse of what seemed to be wooded hillside before a blindfold was tied over his eyes and he was led across rough, sloping ground. When the guy who was leading him barked some kind of order in Italian, he didn't understand, but it must have meant "step up," because right afterwards he stumbled and pitched forward, pulling the kidnapper off-balance. They kind of fell up a couple stairs and lit on a hard, smooth floor. When David struggled to his feet, he had a bumped shin and knee and an awful feeling that the soft thing he'd just stepped rather hard on must have been a bunch of fingers. Blindfolded, he couldn't be sure, of course, but from the noise the guy made when it happened, it probably was something that belonged to him. They went on across the floor, and then the kidnapper said something that must have meant stairs again, only this time there were a lot of them and they were going down—down into something that smelled damp and musty.

"Shut up down there among the ancient bones" —this time the words seemed to explode in David's mind. Too frightened to move, he stood perfectly still, picturing the dark hole under the church's floor so vividly that even when the kidnapper pulled off the blindfold, he couldn't believe he wasn't there. As a matter of fact, for a moment after he saw the place, he still wasn't positive. The stone walls had no windows and there was a dank, underground smell in the air. On the other hand it was much bigger than he'd expected a burial vault to be, and even after he'd followed the first, frantic inspection by a more careful one, he couldn't see anything that looked like ancient bones. Instead there seemed to be a rickety table, a chair, a narrow metal cot, and against one wall a large pile of broken crates and barrels and huge pottery wine jugs. The whole thing was dimly lit by one electric bulb in a funnel-shaped metal shade that hung down from the ceiling in the middle of the room. It all looked like the kind of stuff you might find in the cellar of an Italian farmhouse, and after a minute it occurred to David that that probably was what it was—a cellar.

"David." It was Esther's voice, and David turned in time to see Esther and Blair coming down the stairs. Behind them, one of the kidnappers was closing the heavy wooden door. Still feeling a bit

107

encouraged by the fact that they were in an ordinary cellar instead of a burial vault, David managed to smile at them, which for some reason seemed to make them cry all over again. They ran across the room and threw themselves into his arms. He was just beginning to get them quieted down when the door opened again. All three of the kidnappers were coming down the stairs leading Janie and Amanda.

After they'd taken off Janie's and Amanda's blindfolds, the three men went on standing near the foot of the stairs talking together in rapid Italian. It was the first time David had seen them except by moonlight. All three were dressed in black; black leathery-looking jackets, black pants and heavy black boots. The big one's boots were high and shiny, like riding boots, and the other two were wearing heavy black workmen's shoes with high, lace-up tops. All three of them were wearing hoods of a knitted material that fitted tightly to their heads and necks. Two of the hoods were plain black, but David saw now that the tallest man's hood was dark red with zigzag yellow lines radiating out from around the eyeholes and the triangular opening over his mouth.

The big man in the red mask was doing most of the talking. Gesturing violently and throwing his arms around, he looked and sounded as if he were angry or exasperated. David tried hard to understand, but the rapid speech ran together in a stream of unintelligible sound. At last Red Mask threw up his arms in a kind of "what-the-hell" gesture and stomped up the stairs and out the door, and the two other kidnappers followed him. When the door had been slammed shut and obviously locked with a loud grating noise, David turned his attention to his sisters and brother. It was the first time he had really seen them since it all began, and they all looked absolutely awful.

The three little kids were wearing their pajamas and bathrobes. Their faces were streaked with dirt and tears, their hair was tousled and their eyes were red and puffy. Esther's chin was quivering, and Blair's stare looked blank and bewildered. Obviously the twins were miserable, terrified, and exhausted. It was harder to tell about Janie. Her face was expressionless, except for her enormous round eyes, which glittered with what might be mostly excitement; she wasn't talking, however, which showed that she wasn't altogether herself, either. And Amanda—when David looked at Amanda, she only stared back at him so blankly he wasn't sure if she saw him at all.

Esther was tugging at David's arm. "Are we— are we kidnapped?" she asked.

"I guess we are," he said.

Esther started to cry again, a soft, toneless wail.

Suddenly Janie came to life. "We really are, aren't we?" she said. "Just like that boy in Milan— and Isabella."

David looked quickly at Janie. Her eyes were still enormous, but there was a look in them that he thought he recognized. "Look Janie," he said urgently, "this isn't pretend. Those guys aren't playing games. So don't try anything. Do you understand? Not anything."

Janie nodded. "I know. We have been abducted by a bloodthirsty terrorist, and we are in great danger and peril." David looked at her uneasily, but she looked very serious—maybe just a little bit too serious, but it was hard to tell. Esther was still wailing and, David noticed now, shivering. The air in the cellar was cold and clammy, and Esther's robe wasn't very heavy. David led her over to the cot and put her on it. He pulled up the thick gray blanket and tucked it in around her, and she immediately put her thumb in her mouth and curled up in a ball. Amanda seemed to come out of her trance then, and she brought Blair over and got him to lie down beside Esther. There was only the one cot, so David and Amanda sat down on the edge of it beside the twins. Janie began to walk around the room.

There wasn't much for Janie to examine. She walked around the pile of junk, poking at it now and then with her toe. In one corner of the room there was an arrangement that was obviously meant to be a toilet, a bucket in a box with a round hole in the top. Janie looked at the toilet for a minute before she came back to the middle of the room and climbed up in the one chair by the table. When she leaned forward on the table, it started to slope, and she climbed down and straightened out one of its wooden legs, which seemed about to fall off. Back in the chair she sat quietly staring up the stairs at the heavy door that led out of the cellar.

110

After David stopped thinking about what Janie might be going to do next, he began to notice other things. Now that it was quiet in the cellar, he could hear footsteps overhead, and a metallic hammering noise, and once a clattering sound as if someone had dropped something heavy. David wondered if the kidnappers lived up there, in the house above the cellar. The footsteps and the clanking noises went on for quite a while before the key grated in the lock again, and the kidnappers came back down the stairs.

One of the black hoods came first. He was carrying an armload of something that looked like a bunch of pipes and wire. He had almost reached the bottom of the stairs when somebody screamed. It was Janie. Everybody stared at her, and she screamed again and jumped down from the chair and ran across the room yelling, "Help! Help! I'm kidnapped! Save me! Save me!" While the kidnappers just stood there staring, Janie ran behind the pile of junk, climbed over one end of it, jumped over the toilet and dashed back across the room, throwing her arms around like a crazy person the whole time and yelling. At last she sank down against the farthest wall, with her hands clasped together, making a strange jibbering noise that sounded like a frightened monkey.

The short kidnapper said something in a quiet voice to Janie, as if he were trying to calm her down, but she just went on jibbering. He put down the load of stuff he was carrying and started towards her, but she leaped to her feet with such a blood-curdling shriek that everyone in the cellar jumped about a foot into the air. The short kidnapper backed away from her quickly and stepped into the stuff he'd been carrying, and for a minute or two there was nothing but earsplitting confusion. Esther was wailing again, the short kidnapper was hopping and clanking around trying to get his foot loose, and at the top of the stairs the guy with the red mask was bellowing in a very angry voice. Janie went on shrieking until Red Mask ran down the stairs and grabbed her and shook her hard. *"Silenzio!"* he yelled, and she finally did. Then the other black mask put down the stuff he'd been carrying, and they went away. Janie watched them go with a look on her face that David had seen a lot of times before.

Janie," he said, starting across the room, but Amanda beat him to it. Dashing past him to where Janie was still standing against the wall, she shook her almost as hard as the kidnapper had. "Janie, you idiot. You want to get us all killed?"

Janie trembled her lower lip and her eyes filled up with tears, which might have looked pitiful if you hadn't seen her do it so many times before. "I couldn't help it," she said. "I was hysterical with terror, like Isabella in *The Secret of Holby House.*"

"You were not hysterical. You were just pretending. But those guys aren't pretending, and if you keep on acting crazy they might decide it's too much trouble to keep us alive. You could get us all killed, you little idiot."

She shook Janie again, and Janie's lip trembled

harder and big tears rolled out of the corners of her eyes and down her cheeks. "I wasn't pretending," she said. "I *was* hysterical with terror."

David pulled Amanda away. "Leave her alone," he said. "Come over here. I want to talk to you."

"Look," he said when they were on the other side of the room. "It doesn't do any good to yell at her. I don't think she'll do it again if we explain it to her—about the danger. It's just that when she starts imagining like that, she really isn't pretending. Dad says there's a part of Janie that really believes all her nonsense. There was probably a part of her that really was hysterical with terror."

"Oh yeah," Amanda said. "Look at her. Just look at her." Janie was still standing against the wall. Her face was still wet and shiny with tears, but she was smiling, and the glassy gleam that always meant she was up to something was back in her eyes.

David nodded—and sighed. "And on the other hand," he said, "there was probably another part of her that was having a ball." He sighed again. "I'll talk to her," he said.

twelve

The stuff that one of the kidnappers had gotten tangled up in when Janie started screaming turned out to be a couple of folding metal cots with woven wire springs. David had just started to set them up when the cellar door opened again and one of the black masks came back with an armload of blankets. Actually, he didn't come all the way back. What he did was to come down a few steps and stop to look around. Janie was still standing against the wall at the farthest side of the cellar. The kidnapper looked at Janie for a minute; then he threw the blankets down to the foot of the stairs and went away again.

The cots weren't easy to put together, but finally, with Amanda's help, David managed to get them untangled and made up with mattresses and blankets. They put Janie and Esther to bed in one of them and Blair in another. Amanda wrapped herself up in a blanket and sat down on the third one, but she said there wasn't any use for her to try to sleep because she knew she'd never be able to sleep there, not if she stayed a million years. David didn't think he would either, but it was cold in the cellar so he got in with Blair. It wasn't too comfortable because the springs were so saggy that David immediately sank down into a kind of valley, and Blair rolled down on top of him. He tried pushing Blair back onto his own side several times, but the bed sloped so much he rolled back down. So at last David just decided to make the best of it. He was still telling himself that he probably wouldn't be able to sleep anyway, when suddenly he was waking up feeling as if he'd been asleep for quite a while.

He woke up all at once, going from deep sleep to a full realization of where he was and what had happened with a kind of mental lurch that sent a sharp pain through the lump on his forehead. Opening his eyes a little bit, he looked around. The one dim bulb was still burning inside its metal shade, sending out a pale, shadowy light. In the windowless room it was impossible to tell if morning had come, but some kind of internal clock seemed to be saying that it had. Closing his eyes again, David pictured the villa with the morning sun slanting in through the deep-silled windows—into deserted rooms where the covers were thrown back on empty beds. He imagined the front door opening, and the Thatchers coming in. The Thatchers would have worried faces because it was late and the twins hadn't arrived to spend the day. He could see their faces become more and more worried as they looked into one empty room after the other. Then he saw Andrew's face, round and reddish, but not smiling the way it usually was, as he talked into the telephone. He could see the expression on Andrew's face as he asked for the hotel in Rome where Dad and Molly were staying, and then—as he talked to Dad—telling the awful news.

A lump was starting to form in David's throat again when suddenly Amanda sat up and threw back the covers. Her eyes looked strange, red and puffy, from sleep or perhaps from crying, although David hadn't seen her cry. She looked over at David, and when she saw that he was awake, she did something with her face that you could tell was meant to be a smile. Immediately the lump in his throat got bigger and more painful. He wasn't sure why, except that it really gets to a person when someone who usually isn't very long-suffering suddenly is trying to be brave and cheerful when everything is terrible.

Swallowing hard so that his voice would come out right, David said, "Wait a minute, Amanda." She was headed across the room toward the toilet in a box arrangement that the kidnappers had rigged up. Most of the Stanley family wasn't very strong on modesty, but Amanda definitely was. David had seen her go into a tizzy when even one of the twins barged in on her when she was in the bathroom. David quickly rolled Blair up the slope, crawled out of the sag in the cot, and started arranging some of the old crates and barrels from the pile of junk into a kind of little room for the toilet. As soon as Amanda saw what he was up to, she began to help, and it didn't take them long to get it finished.

When Amanda came back from the bathroom,

David was sitting on her cot because Blair was still asleep in his. She sat down beside him and said, "That was a good idea."

"Thanks," David said. But he didn't say anything more because he was trying to decide whether to ask Amanda something. He finally did decide that it was better to ask her now, if he was ever going to, while she was in an unusually friendly frame of mind. "Oh, Amanda," he said at last, "why did you go out alone last night—to the picnic place?"

She looked at him for such a long time without saying anything that he was about to say, "All right, forget it," when suddenly she stood up and unbuttoned her jacket and got something out of her shirt pocket. She sat back down and smoothed out a wrinkled piece of paper on her knees. On the paper, in stiff, roundish handwriting with little pointy flourishes, it said,

> *Dear Amanda,*
> *Please come to the table of stone for picnics at 10:00 o'clock tonight. I love you.*
>
> > *Sincerely,*
> > *Hilary*

David looked at the note for quite a while before he said, "Hilary didn't write it."

"Look," Amanda said in a normally sarcastic tone of voice, "I don't need you or anybody to tell me that. I *know* Hilary didn't write it."

117

"But you thought he did—last night?" It was a question, and he hoped it sounded like one. He had tried hard to keep it from sounding like, "How could you possibly have thought he wrote it?"

He must not have been entirely successful, because Amanda's lip curled even more, and she said, "No, of course not. I knew all the time that a bunch of lousy kidnappers wrote it. That's why I went out there all by myself in the middle of the night."

David sighed. "Well," he said, "it's just that it's not the way an English-speaking person would arrange the words. An English person would say 'the stone picnic table' instead of 'the table of stone for picnics.' And besides, the handwriting looks so—Italian. You know, kind of round and spiky looking, like the notes that Janie's teacher writes."

Amanda stared at David. "You're crazy," she said. "Do you mean you think Janie's teacher is a kidnapper?"

"No. I didn't mean she wrote it. I just meant her handwriting looks a little like that. It's the way a lot of Italian people write."

Somewhere in the distance there was the sound of a motor. It got louder very rapidly, and then someplace quite near by, it sputtered into silence. Almost immediately afterwards, the footsteps started overhead again. Amanda became very quiet. She sat stiffly still with her shoulders hunched up and followed the sound of heavy boots stomping back and forth with her eyes.

"They're up there again," she whispered.

"Again?" David said. "Do you think they all went away?"

"I don't know, but it's been quiet up there until just now, and it sounded as if someone just arrived."

"Yeah. I guess some of them must have gone away, at least. But I'll bet someone stayed here. I doubt if they'd all go away at once."

Amanda's hunched shoulders twitched. "What do you think they want us for, David? Why did they kidnap us?"

"I don't think they meant to," David said. "At least, not all of us."

She stared at him. "You mean they only meant to kidnap—me?" When she said "me" she winced, as if from a sudden pain.

David hesitated. He didn't want to make her feel worse, but surely she'd already thought about it herself. "Well, the note was just to you. And they only had one cot ready. They didn't know that I was going to follow you and Janie and the twins were going to follow me. But when we all showed up, they just had to take us too, to keep us from spreading the alarm before they had a chance to get away."

Amanda nodded, looking so frightened and miserable that David wished he'd never mentioned it. "Yeah," she said. "I thought of that, but I guess I just didn't want to believe it." She put her face down into her hands. Then she took it out and said, "But why? Why me?"

He shook his head, but after a minute he said, "Amanda, you know you're always—I mean, how

119

you sometimes mention that your father has a lot of money?"

Amanda stopped looking like a whipped puppy and glared at David, and it was a relief to see her looking more like herself. "I don't mention it very often," she said. "And besides, it just so happens to be the truth."

"Well, how many people have you mentioned it to since we came to the villa?"

"Hardly anyone. Except for some of the people at the villa and maybe one or two people at school. But I obviously haven't told anyone Italian, since I don't speak the language. And those guys"—she rolled her eyes upward—"are definitely Italian."

"But someone you told could have told—" David was starting when someone interrupted.

"I might have mentioned it to some Italian people." Janie was sitting up in bed.

"I didn't know she was listening," Amanda said.

"She probably hasn't been for very long," David whispered. "She never lies still after she's awake. I doubt if she could." Dad always said that it exhausted him to even think about the way Janie woke up in the morning, unconscious one second, and all systems go the next. Climbing over Esther, Janie came to where David and Amanda were sitting on Amanda's cot.

"I think I told some people at my school," she said. "Italian kids are very interested in Hollywood and movie stars and things like that, so I just told them a little bit about how your father lives near all the movie stars' houses and about his car and boat and how much money he has."

"Can you remember who it was you told?" David asked.

"Well, I just told this special friend of mine called Anna and her brother, Geppe, but then they wanted me to tell some of their friends and—well, probably most of the kids at the school know about it now."

David groaned. "And hundreds of their friends and relatives," he said.

"Wait a minute," Amanda said. "Whoever the kidnappers are, they had to have known a lot of other stuff besides just about my dad's money. They must have known about Mom and Jeff going away to Rome and—"

"Yeah," David said, suddenly excited, "and about how you—" He stopped and regarded Amanda warily. "—you know—about Hilary. They had to know that you would go out to see Hilary, if you thought he'd written a note asking you to." While he was still talking, David was almost wishing Amanda would get mad again, because if she didn't it would mean she was really not herself at all. But she only nodded, looking worried and scared.

"I know," she said. "It's as if someone who lives at the villa must have helped them."

David nodded.

"Like maybe—Marzia," Amanda said.

"Marzia," David said, amazed. "That's crazy. Marzia wouldn't do anything like that."

"How do you know? She tried to make me think I ought to go back to California."

"Well, if she did, it was only because you both like Hilary. But that doesn't mean she'd try to get you kidnapped."

"Well, maybe she wouldn't on purpose," Amanda said. "But she could have helped the kidnappers by accident. Like maybe they got information from her without her knowing what they were planning."

"But how could that have happened? Italian girls aren't allowed to talk to strange men."

"Well, what if these guys work on the *fattoria* sometimes for her uncle, or something like that. The thing is, someone must have told the kidnappers about me and Hilary, and not too many people know, unless—"she stopped suddenly and looked at Janie.

Janie looked quickly away, hiding her eyes behind her long eyelashes.

"Janie?" David said.

Janie didn't say anything. She was wrapping and unwrapping her thumb with the belt of her bathrobe. "Jane Victoria Stanley. Have you been talking about that, too, at your school? Have you been talking about Amanda—uh—liking Hilary?"

"Well," Janie said. "Only a little. Because Anna was telling me about how her big sister has a boyfriend who lives in Siena, so I just told her that my sister's boyfriend comes all the way from London, and then, when she didn't believe me, I had to tell her a few other things."

"What things?"

"Well, most of it was true—like how they go to school in Florence together every day."

"Wow," David said. "It could be practically the whole town of Valle. What I mean is, nearly everyone in town must know enough stuff to have written the note and everything. Janie, if you'd just keep your mouth shut . . ."

Janie's chin was beginning to wobble, and this time it looked as if she was going to cry for real. David was one of the few people who could tell the difference. But then Amanda said, "Look. It really doesn't matter." Both David and Janie looked at her in surprise. "What I mean is, now that it's happened, it's probably better that a lot of people knew enough to have arranged the kidnapping, because if it could only be a few people, we might guess who they are." She rolled her eyes up toward where the boots were still tromping around. "Because if we guessed and those guys found out, or even if they thought we might be able to guess . . ."

Right away David saw what she meant. If kidnappers think that you know who they are, they aren't ever going to turn you loose, not even if they get the money or whatever it is they want—because they know you'll tell on them. "That's right," he said. "So we mustn't try to see their faces or anything like that, or let them think we know anything about them at all." He looked hard at Janie to be sure she understood.

Janie nodded, looking excited. "Like I shouldn't

123

let them know that I know what their names are?"

"Janie! Do you?"

"Well, not all of their names. I don't know the name of that big one in the red mask, but the middle-sized one is Pietro, and the little one who got his foot tangled up in the bed is named Gino."

"How do you know?"

"I heard them say each other's names when they were talking over there by the stairs."

"What else did they say?" Amanda asked.

"I didn't hear all of it," Janie said. "They weren't talking very loud. Except the big one was angry—about us all being here. I think he was saying that we weren't any good to them—except for Amanda."

David felt the cold prickle again at the back of his neck. A question had come into his mind about what kidnappers did with people who weren't any good to them. He didn't want to think about what the answer might be.

"David, I'm hungry." Esther was awake and sitting up in bed. She looked around the room and began to whimper. David went over to the cot and sat down beside her, and she leaned against him whimpering and asking questions like, "Can we go home now, David? Will they let us go home today? When are we going to have breakfast?"

In between answering Esther with, "I don't know. I don't know," David was thinking hard. He had to decide how much to tell Janie and the twins about their situation. Since he and the kids weren't of any use to the kidnappers because they didn't have any rich parents who could pay a lot of money to get them back alive, they were only going to be a whole lot of extra trouble. And what most people do about extra trouble is try to get rid of it as quickly as possible. So the kidnappers would probably want to get rid of him and the kids, and as far as he could see, there were only two ways they could do that. One way was to turn them loose; but there wasn't much chance they'd do that, at least not until they got their money for Amanda and she could be turned loose, too. The other way, David didn't even want to think about. As far as he could see, the only thing he and the kids could do was to be as little extra trouble as possible so that the kidnappers wouldn't decide that they had to be gotten rid of right away.

That much was easy to figure out. It was easy to see that he had to make sure the kids understood about not being any trouble. What he couldn't decide was whether to tell them why. If he didn't explain it to them, they might not take his warning seriously; on the other hand, if he told them what he was afraid of, they might take it too seriously. Another crying and screaming fit might be just what it took to make the kidnappers decide to get rid of them all—in the quickest way possible.

He was still trying to make up his mind how much to tell the kids when the key grated in the lock. The kidnappers were coming back.

thirteen

David noticed that Esther had stopped whimpering
and when he turned he saw why—the kidnapper on
the stairs, the one Janie had said was called Gino,
was carrying a tray with bowls and dishes on it. He
came down a few steps and stopped and waited while
the other black masked guy came in and locked the
door behind them. David felt relieved that Red Mask
wasn't with them. Before the two kidnappers had
even reached the foot of the stairs, Esther was at the
table. Climbing up on the chair, she dusted off the
table with her hands and then arranged herself neatly
in front of it as if she were waiting for a waiter at a
restaurant.

Gino held the tray, and Pietro took the dishes
off one by one and put them on the table. There was
a large bowl, a cracked ceramic pitcher, some plates
and forks, and a large wine jug that seemed to be
full of water. Esther peeked in the bowl.

"Spaghetti?" she said in a surprised tone of
voice.

The two kidnappers stood over her with their
hooded heads tipped down, like two black vultures

watching something on the ground beneath their tree. Esther looked up at them and nodded. "Spaghetti," she said in a politely informative tone of voice, as if they might have been wondering. Then she turned around towards the cot where Blair was just beginning to wake up. "Blair," she called, "wake up. It's spaghetti for breakfast."

Yawning and rubbing his eyes, Blair padded across the cellar to the table. Standing right in front of the kidnappers, he yawned again so hard that he nearly tipped over backwards; and then, catching his balance, he smiled up at the owlish eyes in the black masks as if they were ordinary faces.

Somehow Blair's smile scared David more than anything else. It showed him what a long way Blair and Esther were from realizing just how much danger they were in. Now that no one was running or yelling, they seemed to think that everything was all right and there wasn't any reason to be frightened anymore. David started for the table, but Janie was there ahead of him.

"Spaghetti?" Janie was saying in an incredulous tone of voice, peeking into the large bowl. "Spaghetti for breakfast?" And then she started saying other things to the kidnappers in Italian. David didn't get very many of the words, but her tone of voice was easy to understand. Janie was obviously unhappy about spaghetti for breakfast, and she was telling the two kidnappers all about it.

"Janie," David said. "Janie! Janie!" He kept saying it louder and louder, but Janie just got louder in Italian, until David practically yelled, "Janie, will you shut up!"

She looked up at him in surprise. "What's the matter?" she asked. "I'm just telling them about balanced diets and vitamin C, and about how I can't help being a fussy eater because I was born with a very particular stomach."

"Well don't," David whispered at her. "Don't tell them anything like that. You mustn't *bother* them."

"I'm not bothering them, I'm just—"

Grabbing her by one arm, David pulled her over to where Amanda was still sitting on the cot; and he didn't turn loose of her until Gino and Pietro were on their way back up the stairs.

While everyone was eating, David kept wondering just how he could make the kids understand about the danger without upsetting them too much. While he and Blair and Esther were eating, that is. Janie took one look at the spaghetti sauce, which was a greenish color and smelled of garlic, and said, "Yick," and refused to eat anything except a few bare strands of spaghetti. Amanda took her share on a plate, but she only picked at it as if she were having trouble swallowing. Janie was nothing to worry about since she often went without eating much; but David wondered if Amanda was getting sick, or if she was only too worried and upset to be hungry. He still hadn't finished deciding what to tell the kids when the kidnappers came back, and this time Red Mask came, too.

Pietro opened the cellar door and held it open while Red Mask came through and swaggered down the steps. Gino closed and locked the door behind him. Watching them, David noticed that Red Mask was not only taller than the other two but also a lot heavier; when he started to talk there was a difference in his voice, too. It sounded deeper and harsher. When he spoke, everyone, including the other kidnappers, listened very carefully. There was something about the harsh voice, the sharp, quick movements, and the angry-looking eyes staring out the center of the yellow zigzags that made him particularly scary. After Gino and Pietro had cleared away the breakfast things and straightened up the broken table leg, Red Mask sat down and leaned across the table staring at each of his captives in turn. When the dark eyes flashed at David, his heart thundered in his chest.

After Red Mask had looked at each one of them in turn, his eyes went back to where Janie was sitting on the middle cot. *"Venite qui!"* he said, motioning with his forefinger.

David caught his breath. Janie hadn't seemed particularly afraid of Gino and Pietro that morning, but Red Mask was different. If she decided to throw another screaming fit. . . . But he needn't have worried—at least not about that. Janie got off the cot and walked slowly towards Red Mask. Partway there, she turned and looked back at David, and he nodded and tried to smile. Behind the table, Red Mask sat stiffly, with the other two kidnappers standing on either side of him. To David it looked like some kind of weird courtroom scene—an evil, hooded judge and jury about to pronounce sentence on. . . . Janie's head and shoulders barely cleared the top of the table. Her bathrobe belt had come untied and was trailing behind her; her robe was hanging down lopsidedly over her pink teddy bear pajamas; and her blond hair was tousled into floppy curls. She looked so completely helpless and innocent that it made a lump in David's throat—and he knew better.

Leaning across the table Red Mask started saying some things in Italian. Janie listened and nodded, and then she turned around and said, "He wants me to translate for him. He wants me to tell you what he's saying." Then she turned back to Red Mask and said, "Okay, *comincia*."

Red Mask talked for quite a long time, and David was able to tell from the tone of his voice and a familiar word now and then, that he was giving them some kind of a warning. When he had finished, Janie translated.

"He says we are their prisoners and we are hidden in a place where no one will ever find us and we must be very good and quiet and not try to escape, and if we do we will be all right and very soon we'll get to go back to our family, but if we are bad or try to get away, something very terrible will happen to us."

"*Avete capito?*" Red Mask shouted, hitting the table with his fist. Everybody jumped, and the table sank down on one side. Gino and Pietro propped the table back up with the broken leg.

"*Avete capito?*" Janie asked. "I mean, do you understand?"

They all nodded. "They all *capiscono*," Janie told Red Mask.

Taking some paper and a pen out of his pocket, Red Mask put them on the table and pointed at Amanda. "*Venite qui*," he said, but Amanda only shrank back against the wall.

"He wants you to come here, too," Janie said.

Amanda looked frantically at David, but he could only shake his head helplessly. Finally she got up and slowly walked to the table, looking very pale and shaky. Red Mask pointed at her and then at the paper and said some more things in Italian. Even before Janie translated, David knew what he wanted.

"He says you have to write a note to your father and tell him that you are kidnapped and that if he ever wants to see you again he must come to Italy immediately and bring a million dollars."

Amanda began to cry. David had never seen her cry before, and she didn't do it easily and naturally the way little kids do. You could tell that she was hating it by the way she held her head straight up and clenched her teeth against the sobs. But her face twitched and quivered, and tears flooded out of her eyes and down her cheeks. "All right," she said finally through her clenched teeth. "Tell him I'll write the letter."

The kidnappers were all staring at Amanda.

Over Red Mask's head, the other two looked at each other, and then quickly back at Amanda. Red Mask tipped back in his chair and looked up at them. Then, leaning forward suddenly across the table, he said something to Amanda that sounded like a question —an angry question.

"He wants to know why you're crying so hard?" Janie said. "He wants to know if your father doesn't really have a million dollars."

Amanda fought against sobs, and David held his breath, wondering what she would say. And— what the kidnappers would do if she told them what David was pretty sure was the truth—that her father didn't have anything like a million dollars.

"Tell them my father has a million dollars," Amanda said at last. She sobbed again, swallowed hard, and caught her breath. "Tell them he'll come and bring them the money."

When Janie had translated to Red Mask, he got up out of the chair and motioned for Amanda to sit down. He spread the paper out in front of her and put the pen on it. Then he put his hands behind his back and began to rock back and forth. He went backwards and forwards, while everyone, including Gino and Pietro, stared at him and waited. Now and then he looked up at the ceiling and then down at the paper. Then, suddenly, he leaned over and jabbed his finger at the top of the paper.

"*Caro Babbo,*" he said.

"He says to write 'Dear Father,' " Janie said.

Amanda wrote, and Red Mask rocked some

more and then pointed at the paper again and said something else—a long sentence this time. But instead of translating right away, Janie tipped her head on one side and bit her lower lip—and right away David began to get a sinking feeling. He got up off the cot and started edging towards the table, just in case. Sure enough, Janie said something to Red Mask that sounded as if she were arguing or else giving advice. Red Mask answered her, and Janie looked surprised and said something back, and Red Mask answered, looking exasperated, and Janie added a few more comments. When Red Mask looked even more exasperated, David got up his nerve and interrupted.

"Janie," he said, "what are you talking about?"

"Well," she said, "he said for me to tell Amanda to write, 'I have been kidnapped by a gang of dangerous men.' So I just asked him if his gang had a name, and he said no they didn't, and I said that I thought all the gangs who kidnap people, at least all the important ones, had names with words like *Army* or *Brigade* in them, and he said his gang didn't, and I said maybe they ought to make up one because it would sound a lot better, like if it got put in the paper or something, and he said he didn't want to make up a name, and I was about to say—"

"Well, don't!" David said. "Just tell Amanda exactly what he said."

Janie sighed. "Well, I just thought—"

"Don't!" David said. "Don't think anything. For heaven's sake, Janie, just tell Amanda exactly what they tell you to."

133

Janie shrugged and said, "Okay. Amanda just write, 'I have been kidnapped by a gang of dangerous men.'" After that David stayed beside the table and listened and watched while Janie translated and Amanda wrote. When it was finished, the letter said:

Dear Father,

I have been kidnapped by a gang of dangerous men. If you ever want to see me again come immediately to Florence with a million dollars. Get a room at the Tuscano Hotel. You will be contacted there with more instructions. Do not say anything to the police.

Please come quickly. I am very frightened.

Your daughter,
Amanda

When Amanda had signed her name, Red Mask leaned over her and read the letter very carefully, pronouncing the English words with a very Italian accent. On the other side of the table Janie stood on tiptoe and read the letter, too.

"Oh, oh," she said suddenly, and pointed to the place on the letter where it said "a million dollars." She motioned for Red Mask to look and started to say something in Italian. David stepped on her foot as hard as he could.

"Ouch," she said, interrupting herself. "You stepped on my foot, David."

"I know it," David said. "What were you saying to him? What were you talking about?"

"I was just going to tell him that he forgot something. He forgot the part about unmarked bills. In kidnap notes you always have to say, 'One million dollars in unmarked bills.' "

"Janie." David kept his voice calm and quiet, but he tried to make his eyes threaten everything he could think of. "Come over here and let me see your foot. Let me see if I hurt it."

Janie let herself be led over to the cot. She sat down on the edge, and David took off her shoe. As he pretended to examine her toes, he whispered, "What do you want to tell them stuff like that for?"

"I was just trying to help—"

"Help! What do you want to help them for? Whose side are you on, anyway?"

Janie looked thoughtful. "Yeah," she said. "I see what you mean. What we ought to be doing is trying to trick them—"

"No, no." David's whisper got more high-pitched. "No tricks. No tricks on anybody. Please Janie, don't try any tricks."

Janie nodded. "Okay," she said, "no tricks." But her eyes had that glassy look, and David knew from experience there probably wasn't much connection between what she was saying and what was going on in her head.

Either Red Mask didn't understand what Janie had been talking about, or else he just didn't care about unmarked bills. He seemed to be satisfied with the note the way it was. He folded it very carefully and went up the stairs with Gino and Pietro following him. After they'd gone, Amanda sat at the table for a long time with her head down on her arms.

fourteen

After the kidnappers went away with the ransom note, Amanda went on crying for a long time. She eventually got up from the table, went over to her cot and lay down on her stomach with her face hidden in her arms, still crying. At first the little kids hung around looking at her and at each other with worried faces. They hadn't ever seen Amanda crying, and they weren't sure if they should try to cheer her up or not.

They certainly would have tried if it had been anyone else, but she'd been their sister long enough for them to know you couldn't treat Amanda the way you did other people. After a while she raised her head long enough to tell them to go away, so they did. Then quite a while later she sat up and rubbed her face hard on the sleeve of her jacket and went over and sat down by David. The little kids had gone over behind the pile of junk in the corner. Amanda checked to be sure they were out of hearing and then said, "I have to tell you something."

Feeling pretty sure he knew what it was going to be, David nodded.

"It's about my father," Amanda said. "He won't come and bring the money."

"Yeah," David said. "I kind of thought he didn't really have a million dollars."

She nodded. "He makes a lot of money, but I think he spends it almost as fast as he makes it. I know he doesn't have a million dollars, but he might possibly be able to get that much by borrowing and selling some things, like his boat, but I doubt it. But it isn't just that. What it is, is—" She stopped and clenched her teeth and scowled. It looked as if she were very angry, but David realized that it wasn't so much anger as an attempt to keep from crying again. "It's just that he probably wouldn't come even if he had millions of dollars lying around all over everywhere. It just probably won't"—she stopped and scowled again—"it won't make that much difference to him."

The last few words came out very shaky, and then she put her face down in her hands, and her shoulders began to shake. David felt awful. Trying to think of something that would cheer her up, he finally said something very dumb. What he said was, "But you were always talking about how crazy your father was about you and how he gave you expensive presents all the time—like the crow and all the snakes and everything."

Amanda nodded and cried harder than ever. It was a long time before she was able to talk, and when she finally was, she began to tell David about how she hadn't really been lying to him about her father.

138

What she had really been doing was lying to herself —trying to make herself believe that her father did love her and that he would have let her come and live with him except that the court said she had to stay with Molly. But all the time she really knew that he didn't like having her there very much and was probably relieved when she went home after her visits.

"He probably wouldn't have me there at all if he didn't know Mom would love for me to quit visiting him. He only lets me come and buys me all that expensive junk to make her angry."

David thought of trying to convince Amanda that what she said wasn't true, but he really thought it might be, and he doubted if he could sound very convincing. The only thing he could think of to say was, "Well, your mom really loves you. I know that."

Amanda nodded. "I know. I used to blame her for the divorce and tell myself she was going to stop loving me just the way she stopped loving my father, but I guess I always knew it wasn't true. But she doesn't have a million dollars or anything like it, and"—Amanda looked over towards where the little kids were playing and lowered her voice—"my father is not going to show up with the money, and what's going to happen to all of us then? And it will all be my fault."

She cried some more, and David tried to think up comforting things to say, most of which turned out to be pretty useless. After she was calm again, he asked her why she'd told Janie to tell the kidnappers that her father would bring the money.

She shrugged. "I was afraid of what they would do if they knew there wasn't going to be any money."

"But they're going to find out eventually."

Amanda nodded. "But at least this gives us a little time, and maybe something will happen. Maybe the police will find us or—"

"Yeah," David said nodding eagerly. "You're right." Time was important. Time for something to happen, or maybe even—just time for the kidnappers to get to know them all better. "Yeah," he said again thoughtfully. "Like King Tut."

"King Tut?" Amanda said, but then after she'd thought about it for a minute she said, "Oh, I see what you mean."

King Tut was the turkey that old Mr. Golanski had given Dad for Thanksgiving dinner last year. Only Mr. Golanski had made the serious mistake of bringing Tut to the Stanleys while he was still alive, and by the time Thanksgiving came everyone had had time to get to know him. As a result King Tut was still strutting around—at the moment back at Mr. Golanski's where he was having his room and board paid by the Stanleys until they got back from Italy—which Mr. Golanski, being a farm person all his life, thought was pretty ridiculous.

But the point about King Tut was that having a chance to get acquainted with the Stanley kids might have more or less the same effect on the kidnappers. After all, it did seem that a bunch of little kids ought to be at least as appealing as a turkey.

But then, of course, there *was* Janie. Getting

140

better acquainted with Janie might have the opposite effect. David had to admit that there had been times when he'd wanted to wring her neck himself, and he was her own brother.

The thing for him to do, he decided after thinking it over, was to do everything he could to get everyone to look and act as good as possible, so that the kidnappers couldn't help noticing how cute and appealing and good they all were. Because if they really noticed, perhaps it would occur to them how much better they'd feel, when the kidnapping was all over, if the Stanley kids were all in more or less the same condition. But when David explained what he'd been thinking to Amanda, she wasn't at all sure it would work that way.

"They're kidnappers," she said. "What do they care about people." But later on, when David started trying to make the kids look a little more appealing, she offered to help.

It had been very dirty in the back of the kidnap truck, and it wasn't exactly clean in the cellar, and everyone was looking pretty grungy, so it seemed as if the first step would be to clean everyone up as much as possible. The only water available was the drinking water in the wine jug. It was cold, but it would have to do. In the pile of debris in the corner, David found the bottom half of a big pottery wine jug, which made a pretty good wash basin. Using the end of his bathrobe belt as a washcloth, he and Amanda washed first their own hands and faces and then the little kids'. Fortunately, Amanda had a comb

141

in her jeans' pocket, so while David washed, she combed. When they had finished, everyone certainly looked a lot neater, and perhaps, David thought hopefully, cuter and more appealing. But the next time the kidnappers came in they didn't seem to notice, and soon afterwards Janie started a game of building a fort out of stuff from the junk pile, and Blair and Esther got interested and joined in, and before long they were as dirty as ever. So David went back to trying to think of some other ways to keep the kidnappers from getting rid of the Stanleys in the way he didn't even want to think about.

There was, of course, escape. Red Mask had warned them about what he would do to anybody who tried to get away. David tried to remember exactly what Red Mask had said. If he remembered correctly, Janie had translated Red Mask's threat only as "something terrible." He thought of asking Janie just what Red Mask had threatened to do to an escaper, but he decided it wouldn't be a good thing to remind her of. He'd just have to risk it, without knowing what the consequences would be if he got caught. Because he was definitely thinking about it.

He was thinking about it early the next morning. He guessed it was morning, anyway, because the last meal had seemed to be a dinner, and then for a long time, several hours at least, it had been perfectly quiet on the floor above. There had been a motor noise going away into the distance shortly after the last meal, and it had been quiet ever since.

What if everyone had gone away? And what if the lock on the cellar door could be picked? It was probably a very old lock without anything like a deadbolt or any other complicated mechanism. Getting out of bed, David rummaged around in the junk pile until he found an old rusty nail that he'd remembered seeing there. Everyone else seemed to be fast asleep.

It was the first time he'd been on the stairs since he'd staggered down them blindfolded the night before. In the silence the old wood creaked under his feet alarmingly. Several times he stopped to listen, but except for the creak of the stairs when he shifted his weight, he heard nothing at all.

At the top of the stairs, he reached up and very carefully turned the old handle-type door latch—just to be sure it hadn't been left unlocked the night before by accident. But no such luck. The latch went down about half an inch and stopped. The door held. The keyhole was just below the latch. Biting his lip and holding his breath, David poked the nail into the keyhole and started prying, first in one direction and then in another. After a moment the nail caught, and the lock seemed to be starting to give. David pressed a little harder—and then something in the keyhole flipped over, the nail fell out of David's hand, and the door was jerked wide open. Standing in the doorway, two steps above him, was a huge hairy man wearing nothing but a pair of boxer shorts—and a red mask.

It was absolutely the most terrifying thing that could possibly happen—like jumping into a deep

143

hole and finding it was full of cobras, or looking out your bedroom window and seeing a werewolf looking in at you. David stared up into the hooded face for what seemed like a lifetime before his shocked mind got the message to his feet. When he finally got turned around and started down the stairs, Red Mask grabbed him. Twisting his arm up behind his back until it seemed about to snap, Red Mask pushed him down the stairs and across the room. Near the cots, he turned David around to face him, took hold of his shoulders and squeezed so hard David thought he felt bones breaking. Then he shook him slowly back and forth, lifted him up and dropped him in a heap on the floor. David covered his head with his arms, thinking he was going to be hit or kicked, but nothing more happened. When he looked up, Red Mask was going back up the stairs.

That was all. During the whole thing neither of them had said a word. No one else even woke up. Later, David had a bunch of purple bruises on his shoulders and a sore arm—and no more plans about escaping.

fifteen

In the cellar there was no way to tell day from night. The one dim bulb in the funnel-shaped shade shone continuously. The only clue to the time of day was when the kidnappers brought food, and the long periods when things got very quiet on the floor above and no one came into the cellar, as if the kidnappers had gone away or perhaps gone to sleep. During the periods that were probably daytime, there were frequent noises overhead, footsteps and other sounds. From time to time it sounded as if someone were approaching or going away in a very noisy car or truck. At times the motor noise grew gradually louder and stopped someplace nearby, and at others it started up suddenly with a loud roar and then diminished into the distance.

David slept very little, and then for only short periods. Most of the time he spent worrying. He thought a lot about Dad and Molly and how sad and frightened they must be; and of course he worried about himself and the rest of the kids and what was going to happen to all of them.

By the second day the novelty of the cellar had

really worn off, and Blair and Esther had several crying spells about wanting to go home. Even Janie cried once or twice before David thought of asking her to help, especially with Blair and Esther. After that she switched from being the poor, hysterical kidnap victim to being the brave, resourceful underground organizer.

What David wanted her to do was keep the twins occupied and cheerful—a natural for Janie. She was always able to make a game out of anything, and even in the cellar, where there wasn't much to play with, she did a great job. First she and the twins rowed down jungle rivers in a packing crate and burrowed through the junk pile pretending they were the rabbits from *Watership Down*. Then the next day they built a hideout in the corner, out of crates and boxes, and from then on they had some kind of game going back there nearly all the time. After that the little kids almost stopped crying for home, except at night.

But the other thing Janie insisted on organizing wasn't all that helpful—and that was escape schemes. After his experience, David had no use for them. But she kept coming up with a new idea several times a day, and they were all pretty wild. Like digging a pit trap at the foot of the steps for the kidnappers to fall into, or breaking the light bulb and then clobbering them when they came downstairs in the dark. Every time David talked her out of one of her ideas, she was very disappointed for a while; and then, before very long, she'd come up with another one.

Although David had quit thinking about escape plans, he couldn't stop thinking about what the kidnappers were going to do when they found out there wasn't going to be any money. He thought about it most of the time until about the fourth day after the kidnapping, when something happened that gave him something else to think about.

It began with the motor noise starting up outside and fading away—apparently someone had left the hideout. David noticed particularly because it was between lunch and dinner, and usually the sounds of people arriving and departing happened before breakfast and after dinner. In fact, he and Amanda had been developing a theory about the schedule. The theory was that Gino and Pietro were in charge of the hideout and the captives during the day, and when the motor noises started after dinner it meant that they were going away for the night and Red Mask was arriving. There were some definite clues. For one thing Gino and Pietro were always the ones who served the meals and did other chores around the cellar, such as emptying the toilet. And David certainly had good reason to suspect that Red Mask slept at the hideout during the night. Of course there had been times when all three of them had been there at once, but that seemed to happen only on special occasions, like when the ransom note was written.

David was still thinking about the out-of-phase motor noise when the door of the cellar opened and one of the black masks came in alone. It was Gino, the smallest one. Closing and locking the door behind him, he sat down on the top step and stayed there, just watching as if he were looking at animals at the zoo. Hunched over up there near the ceiling, black and shiny and faceless, he looked like some kind of weird bird of prey, and for a while his presence made David uneasy.

Amanda hardly noticed him, however, and after the first few minutes, the little kids seemed to get used to being watched and went back to playing with some ants they'd found crawling up the wall in the corner. David remembered then about the King Tut theory and wished he'd insisted on cleaning everyone up more recently. He was beginning to think about what the kids might do to look more cute and appealing, when suddenly Gino said, *"Janie, venite qui."*

David didn't dare tell her not to, so Janie climbed up the stairs and for a long time she perched up there beside the kidnapper and chatted away as if he were an old friend. Hoping desperately she was being appealing, and that she wasn't saying things she wasn't supposed to, David listened intently, picking up a few words and phrases now and then that meant something to him, but not enough to really get the drift of the conversation—and kicking himself mentally for not working harder at his Italian.

Then the motor sound began again, in the distance at first and then getting closer, and Gino got up quickly and went out. As soon as he had gone, David pounced on Janie and demanded that she tell him everything that had been said.

"Well," Janie said. "We were mostly talking about movies. Gino likes movies a lot. He wanted to know about movies I've seen, and if I'd seen *Guerra Stellare*, you know, *Star Wars*, and if I liked it. And if I'd ever seen any movie stars, and then Gino asked me if—"

David interrupted. "You didn't call him Gino, did you?"

"No, of course not. I remembered what you said about not knowing who they are so we can't tell on them after they let us loose."

"But if you think of him as Gino, you might forget and call him that when you're talking to him."

Janie looked offended. "I won't forget. A person with an IQ of one hundred and forty-five doesn't forget about things like not calling kidnappers by their names. When a person with an IQ of one hundred and forty-five talks to a kidnapper, she simply asks him a lot of questions so he'll make a mistake and tell her some clues that give away secrets, like where their hideout is, or what they're planning to do next."

"Janie, no! That's just what we don't want to do. We don't want to know their names or who they are or anything else about them. And we don't want any *clues*. Because if they should make a mistake and let something slip out, they'll probably realize it afterwards; and then they'll never let us go—at least not *alive*. Is that what you want to have happen?"

"No." Janie finally looked as if she might really be beginning to take what David was saying seriously.

"Look, Janie. If he makes you talk to him again, don't ask him any questions at all. Just talk to him about—about us. Tell him about what a great family we have and how our parents must be worried to death, and how bad it is for little kids like Blair and Esther to be away from their parents for so long. Talk a lot about Blair and Esther. You know, about how young they are, and how everyone thinks they're so cute, and how some people think Blair looks like an angel."

"Okay. But I guess I'd better not tell him about how Blair has things like ESP sometimes, because then he might guess that Blair knows who they are."

"Blair knows who who are?" David asked.

Janie giggled. "You sound like an owl," she said. "You said who who," and she giggled some more.

"Knock it off, Janie. This is serious. Blair knows who—I mean, who is it that Blair knows who they are?"

"The kidnappers. But don't worry. *You* don't have to know. *I'm* not going to tell who they are. And you know how Blair is. He won't tell you either unless you ask him."

David was beginning to feel as if something in his head was flying into pieces. Grabbing Janie he shook her and said, "Tell me! Who are they?" in a frantic-sounding whisper.

Janie pulled away from him, looking indignant. "You just said you didn't want to know who they were."

"I said we shouldn't try to find out who they are," David said. "Who are they?"

Janie's face took on her maddening "I-can't-believe-how-dumb-ordinary-people-can-be" expression. "David, for someone who's twelve years old, you aren't very logical sometimes. You just said—"

"Look, Janie. I don't want to know what I just said. I want to know who they are."

"Well, okay, but remember, it's your fault. You *made* me tell you. Blair says they're Marzia's brothers. At least two of them are. I don't think Blair knows about that other one—the one in the red mask.

"Marzia's brothers. How does Blair know that?"

"How do I know how Blair knows things? But after he told me, I remembered that Marzia said one of her brothers was named Gino. And I'm not sure but I think she mentioned a Pietro, too."

David felt absolutely stunned. He and Amanda had fooled around with the idea that Marzia had been responsible for giving information to the kidnappers—perhaps by accident—but it had never occurred to him that they might be her brothers. He'd known that Marzia had brothers—several of them—but he'd thought of them as being kids. He remembered now that two of them were older than she was, but he was sure they were only a little older. Like maybe around fifteen or sixteen. And the kidnappers were men—or were they. With the hoods it was hard to tell.

Other clues began to pop into his head. If two of the kidnappers were Marzia's brothers, that would certainly explain how they knew so much about the Stanley family—like the fact that Dad and Molly were away, and that Amanda would probably go out to meet Hilary if he asked her to.

Then there were other things. There were the small trucks that had been parked near the house where Marzia's family lived—the kind of truck that had been used in the kidnapping. And the motorcycles. Now that he thought about it, he realized that the loud motor noises they'd been hearing just outside the hideout were more like motorcycles than like cars, or even trucks. And hadn't Olivia said something about Marzia's brothers having motorcycles?

When you put it all together, it did seem to fall into a pattern. There was even what Olivia had said about the Lino family being very poor since their father had died, and how they all hated living with their uncle and depending on his charity. So that was one more reason to believe the brothers might be willing to do almost anything to get some money— like maybe even a kidnapping.

"You stay here," David said to Janie, and he went over to where Blair was sitting on a box on the other side of the cellar. He was still playing with the ants, making a little bridge out of sticks for them to get up on the box where he'd put a little pile of bread crumbs.

"Blair," David said, "what makes you think the kidnappers are Marzia's brothers?"

Blair looked up and smiled. He put another stick on the bridge and then stood up slowly. Looking very thoughtful he nodded. "They are," he said. "Didn't you know?"

"No, I don't know who they are. How do you know?"

Blair's face puckered into a puzzled expression. "I don't know," he said. "I just know."

"And how about the big one? Who is he?"

Blair hardly ever frowned, but this time he did something that was definitely a frown. "I don't like him," he said. "I don't like that one." And that was all. David went on asking questions, but he wasn't able to find out anything more from Blair.

Although, to David, it seemed terribly important to find out if the two kidnappers really were Marzia's brothers, Amanda didn't agree at all. When David told her, she listened without making any comments until he was all finished, and then she said, "I told you Marzia didn't like me."

"I don't think this proves anything about Marzia," David said. "In fact, if they are her brothers, it just proves that they could easily have gotten all the information they needed without anyone really telling them anything. They probably overheard Ghita and Marzia talking about all of us lots of times."

Sitting hunched over on the end of her cot, Amanda barely seemed to hear what David was saying.

"Don't you think so?" David asked.

She shrugged. "What difference does it make who they are? Whoever they are, they're kidnappers, aren't they?"

Now that he knew, David couldn't see why he hadn't noticed a lot sooner that both Gino and Pietro were very young. Of course, the hoods made it difficult to tell, and they were as tall as some grown men, but there were other things he could have noticed— their hands and wrists, for instance, the pitch of their voices, and even the way they moved. It seemed very obvious now, especially when you compared them to Red Mask, who was not only taller, but thicker, louder, angrier, and a whole lot more frightening.

When Gino and Pietro came down to the cellar the next morning, David observed them very carefully. The little kids ran to the table, as usual, and stood around it watching as Pietro took the breakfast off the tray. This time it was only bread and fruit and cheese. As soon as she saw the food, Esther started whining and telling Janie to say they wanted some scrambled eggs.

"Tell them I always have scrambled eggs for breakfast," Esther whined. "And hot chocolate. Tell them we all want some hot chocolate." And, in spite of David's warning about not being nuisances, Janie translated exactly what Esther had said, complete with the whining tone of voice. But this time David didn't try to make her stop, because he was too involved in watching Gino and Pietro and wondering if they really were Marzia's brothers—and if they were, what difference it might make. What he decided first was that he needed to have a conference with the kids as soon as possible.

After breakfast David did some more planning and then, although he was pretty sure it would be useless, he tried to talk things over with Amanda. It seemed as if every day she got more withdrawn and sad. She was curled up under the covers on her cot now, where she'd been spending most of her time lately. As he sat down beside her, she sat up and seemed to be listening. But when he was through she only shrugged and curled back up again. So David decided to go ahead with the conference without her. He had to do something. In fact, looking at Amanda's wide open eyes, staring at nothing, he felt more strongly than ever that he had to do something—and soon. There were dangers, of course. There were always dangers when Janie was involved in anything. And they had been so firm in rejecting all of her escape plans, he didn't know what her reaction would be to his. Yet, he had to try.

The little kids were behind the junk pile in the little room they'd made from crates and boxes. They were playing some kind of game about man-eating ants, and right at first David had a hard time getting their minds off the game and onto what he was trying to tell them.

The first thing he talked about was Gino and

Pietro and how important it was not to say anything to them about their being Marzia's brothers. He wasn't too worried about Blair saying anything, and Janie apparently understood why it mustn't be mentioned—but he wasn't too sure about Esther. However, Esther seemed to understand, too.

"Janie already told me all about that," she said. "Janie said they won't let us go home if we know who they are. When are they going to let us go home, David?"

"I don't know," David said, "but that's what I want to talk to you about. I've been thinking about this plan." And he went ahead and told them all about his King Tut theory, or at least one version of it. The way he put it to the kids was that if they were particularly cute and charming and good, the kidnappers might get sort of fond of them and decide to let them go. He didn't say anything about King Tut, however, because it didn't seem like a good idea to remind the kids of what would have happened to the turkey if the Stanleys *hadn't* gotten fond of him.

While David was explaining, he noticed that Janie was listening very enthusiastically. Her eyes got very round and almost stopped blinking, and she kept nodding her head and giving a little bounce now and then. "I see what you mean," she said, when he'd finished explaining everything. "I think it's a very good idea."

Actually all David had meant was that Esther should stop whining at the kidnappers and that Janie should stop criticizing and giving advice and that they should all be as polite and clean and good-natured as possible. He was pretty sure the kids intended to follow his suggestions, but he might have done more checking into just how they were going about it, if it hadn't been for Amanda.

When the conference was over and David came out of the corner behind the junk pile, he found that Amanda was crying again; and for the next two or three hours, he didn't have any time to pay attention to what the kids were doing. Instead he sat down on the side of Amanda's cot and tried to get her to stop crying and talk to him. At first she went on sobbing steadily with a kind of hopelessness that was really frightening—as if she were about to lose control of herself completely. David couldn't think what to do except to go on trying to get her to talk to him. At last she did start talking, and once she did, she couldn't seem to stop that either. Most of the time what she said didn't seem to have much to do with why she'd been crying. At least, she hardly mentioned the kidnapping. Instead she just told David all about things that had happened a long time ago, before her parents' divorce—things you could tell she'd been feeling bad about for a long time.

While they were talking, he was vaguely aware of noises in the corner, Janie's voice mostly, but at the time he was too interested in Amanda's problems to pay much attention. He did notice that Janie came out once and got the wash basin and some water, and another time she asked if she could get the comb out of Amanda's jacket pocket. The jacket was lying on the floor near Amanda's cot, and Janie fished around in the pocket for a moment and then disappeared again behind the junk pile. But David didn't even suspect what she was up to until Gino and Pietro came in with the noontime meal.

The kids didn't rush out to meet them and crowd around the table commenting and criticizing the way they usually did. Gino and Pietro put the food on the table and were starting to ask David something about the kids when all of a sudden Janie came out from behind the pile of boxes. She was skipping and holding the bottom of her bathrobe out on each side, and when she got to the center of the room, she stopped and did a sort of curtsey. David noticed then that her hair was combed and her face was clean, except that she had a big blob of smeary lipstick around her mouth and two more round patches of lipstick on her cheeks. Smiling in a very exaggerated way, she looked all around the room as if there were a big audience, and then she curtsied again, and said, " 'The Death of Juliet' by William Shakespeare." Then she pulled the tail of her bathrobe up over her head like a monk's hood and said, "Alack, alack, what blood is this, which stains the stony entrance of this sepulchre?"

During the time that Janie had been going through her Juliet phase that summer, she'd memorized a whole lot of the last scene of *Romeo and Juliet*, and apparently she hadn't forgotten any of it. She went on for quite a long time, pulling her bathrobe up around her head when she was being Friar

158

Laurence, and dropping it down again and making her voice high and squeaky when she was supposed to be Juliet.

Gino and Pietro seemed interested. At least they stood perfectly still and stared at Janie, although, since it was all in English, and Shakespearean English at that, they probably hadn't the faintest idea what was going on.

Janie was down on her knees pretending to kiss the dead Romeo and saying the part about kissing Romeo's lips in case there might still be some poison on them so she could die, too, when David realized what was coming next. Oh, oh, he thought, and he started to get to his feet, but it was too late. Grabbing a butter knife off the lunch tray, Janie shouted, "Oh happy dagger. This is thy sheath," and stabbed herself.

David had gotten so used to Janie's 'dying Juliet bit' last summer that he'd quit paying much attention, but now seeing it through Gino and Pietro's eyes, he had to admit it was pretty impressive. Gino even lunged forward once as if to take the knife away from her, but Pietro must have realized that she couldn't really hurt herself with a butter knife, and he grabbed Gino and held him back. So no one interfered, and Janie went on whooping and screaming and gurgling and kicking until she was through dying, and then she got up and curtsied again and skipped back behind the junk pile.

For a second act all three kids came skipping out singing the Mickey Mouse Club song, holding their hands behind their heads to represent Mickey Mouse ears. Janie had painted the twins' lips and cheeks with Amanda's lipstick, too, and they really looked unusual, to say the least. When they finished the song, Janie lined them up and said, "One-two-three," and they all started trying to do a tap dance routine that Janie had taught herself a long time before by watching old Shirley Temple movies on the TV. After the first few steps Blair mostly watched Janie's feet and did a few little quick shuffles, trying to catch up, but Esther was doing surprisingly well until, just as they were starting to dance off stage, she tripped on her shoestring and fell down and started crying Janie came dancing back out and pulled Esther to her feet and said, "Come on, Tesser. Dance off the stage," but Esther just braced herself and wouldn't move and went on crying. Janie kept tugging until Esther got angry and took a sock at Janie and said, "Leave me alone. I don't want to dance anymore. I want to eat lunch."

So, of course, Janie hit her back, and Esther hit Janie again and ran. She ran around the table with Janie right behind her with her fist in the air. When Esther ducked behind Gino and Pietro, Janie skidded to a stop right in front of them. She jerked her fist down and did a very quick cat-that-ate-the-canary smile, and then she curtsied again and danced backwards, smiling harder all the time, until she disappeared behind the boxes.

Esther came out from behind Gino and Pietro still dripping tears but looking very pleased with herself. She climbed up in the chair and took a bowl of soup off the tray—and in a minute she was whining about the soup being all cold.

As far as David was concerned, that was pretty much the end of the King Tut plan. They went back to the same old scene. Esther whined, Janie gave advice, and Amanda sat around like a zombie. Even worse, Blair took to just standing and staring at the kidnappers in a way even David found unnerving. There wasn't much chance that any of them would come off as appealing.

sixteen

It was during another long quiet period a night or two later that Blair had the dream about the Blue Lady. The Blue Lady was what Blair called the statue of the Virgin that stood in the little niche on the landing of the front staircase in the villa. He'd taken a special interest in it from the day he first saw it, and he talked about it a lot. At least, a lot for Blair, who didn't ordinarily talk very much about anything.

Everyone in the cellar had been asleep, and David was just beginning to wake up. He'd been lying there, half-awake—wondering if it were morning yet and thinking how, if he ever got out of that cellar, he'd always remember to appreciate having nights and days that looked different from each other—when Blair sat up very suddenly, pulling off all the covers.

"What are you doing?" David asked, whispering because everyone else seemed to be sleeping. Blair didn't answer. Instead, he just scrambled over David's stomach and ran across the room toward a box sitting against the wall in the corner of the cellar. When he got to the box, he stood there staring at it for a moment, and then he moved it and looked behind it, and then all around it on the floor, as if he'd lost something. He came back to the bed looking puzzled and thoughtful.

"What is it?" David asked. "What were you looking for?"

"The Blue Lady," Blair said. "Where did she go?"

"The Blue Lady? Do you mean that statue on the stairs at home?"

Blair nodded slowly. "Like that," he said. "Only she was right there on that box, but when I sat up to see her better, she went away."

"You must have been dreaming."

Blair thought for a moment before he said, "What is dreaming?"

That was a hard one to explain, especially to Blair, who never seemed to take much interest in the meaning of words like "actually" and "imagine" or even "real" and "not real." "Well," David said, trying to think of a way to put it that would make it clear to Blair. "Dreaming is what happens at night when you're lying in your bed, only when you open your eyes it isn't happening any more."

Blair nodded, looking as if that cleared it all up for him. "Oh," he said, "that's dreaming."

"See," David said, "you were asleep, and you dreamed that the Blue Lady was on the box."

Blair looked pleased. "I was dreaming the Blue Lady was on the box," he agreed. But then he asked, "Didn't you see her, David?"

Later on, when the others were all awake, David heard Blair asking Esther if she'd seen the Blue Lady; so David had to explain to them all about Blair's dream. They all talked about it for a while—about Blair's dream and dreams in general. All of them, that is, except Amanda, who still wasn't taking any interest in anything. While the rest of them discussed Blair's dream, Amanda just sat on her cot with her face in her hands, and you couldn't tell if she had even heard the conversation.

It was that same day, right after lunch, that they all heard the sound of a motorcycle, and everyone stopped what they were doing and watched the stairs. They all knew by now that when a motorcycle came in the middle of the day, it was Red Mask. Sure enough, a few minutes later he came down the stairs. This time the dark eyes in the center of the radiating yellow zigzags looked angrier than ever. He jerked the chair away from the table, sat down and hit the table with his fist. As Pietro grabbed the broken leg and propped the table back up, Red Mask yelled, *"Venite qui,"* at Amanda.

Janie, with her eyes wide and frightened looking, said, "He wants you to come here, Amanda."

As she got up off her cot and crossed the room, Amanda's face was so stiff and white that David wondered if she might be going to faint. Before she'd even reached the table, Red Mask began to rant and rave at her in Italian. Waving his hands and shaking his finger at Amanda, he went on yelling for quite a

164

long time before he leaned back in the chair and waved his arm at Janie.

But this time Janie only stood there, looking back and forth from Amanda to Red Mask in a confused, worried way. It wasn't until Red Mask prompted her by repeating some phrases, that she began to translate. "He says that you were lying to him about your father being a millionaire, or else your father is lying," she said hesitantly. "He says your father is coming to Italy, and he called a newspaper in Florence and had them print a message in the paper." Janie stopped and looked at Red Mask uncertainly, and after he prompted her, she went on. "The message said that your father was bringing some money for the kidnappers, but it isn't even half a million dollars and it was all that he could get." Janie stopped again, and Red Mask shouted at her, and she went on hurriedly. "He says that he is very angry, and you must write another note saying that your father must get the million dollars if he wants to see you ever again."

Looking at Red Mask's angry eyes and listening to him shout, David felt very frightened; but when he looked at Amanda, his fright became mixed with confusion. Considering the circumstances, Amanda had a very strange expression on her face. It wasn't a smile, but it looked as if it might be getting ready to be one. "My father is on his way to Italy?" she asked Janie.

"That's what he said," Janie told her.

"Are you sure? Ask him if he's sure."

Janie asked Red Mask, and he nodded curtly and then began to say more threatening-sounding things; but Amanda hardly seemed to be listening. She went on acting as if her mind were on something else all the time she was writing the new note.

After the kidnappers had gone away with the second ransom note, everyone, that is nearly everyone, felt depressed. David had been telling the little kids that almost enough time had gone by for Amanda's father to get to Italy, and that they all might be allowed to go home very soon. And now it seemed certain that nothing was going to happen soon—and maybe not at all. Suddenly everything seemed a lot worse. Esther had a crying spell about being hungry and dirty and went around and around the table wailing that she wanted scrambled eggs and clean pajamas and her toy vacuum cleaner. Blair had a crying spell because Janie slapped him for accidentally stepping on her favorite ant; and Janie had a crying spell because David shook her for slapping Blair. David was sitting on a cot thinking about having a crying spell himself, when Amanda sat down beside him and began to talk about making plans. Because Amanda had not been planning or talking, or doing much of anything for quite a while, it surprised him enough to make him forget about crying, at least for the time being.

"I've been thinking about what we can do," Amanda said. Her face was still pale, but her expression was more normal than it had been since the kidnapping. She looked over at the little kids and lowered her voice. "I think there's something that might work," she whispered.

The minute Amanda started whispering, Janie, who had been pouting under the covers on her cot, came out from under the blankets like a jack-in-the-box. A whisper was one thing that Janie absolutely couldn't resist. Dad always said that if Janie were stone cold dead and somebody started whispering, she would immediately come back to life, at least for long enough to get in on the secret. She was halfway across the room before Amanda could say any more.

"Get out of here, Janie," Amanda said. "Go away." And David couldn't help feeling relieved to hear her sounding so much like her old self.

"I want to hear your plan," Janie said. "Why can't I hear the plan, David? I'm supposed to be helping."

"Why can't Janie hear the plan?" David asked.

"Because it would ruin it. This plan depends on not many people knowing about it."

It took quite a bit more argument before Janie gave up and went back to pouting and Amanda went on. "It's about that dream that Blair had," she said. "It made me remember a movie I saw on television. It was about some kids in Italy who saw a vision of the Virgin Mary in a vacant lot, and when they started telling people about it, everyone believed in it and pretty soon they built a shrine. Then the television people came and all sorts of officials and pilgrims from all over Europe. If we could convince those thugs that Blair had had a vision of the Virgin Mary, maybe they'd be—" She stopped and waited to see if David was beginning to catch on.

"Yeah," he said. "It might make them—like, repent, or something."

"Well, I don't know about repent, but I'll bet it'd scare the hell out of them," Amanda said. "And they just might not be so quick to decide to bump us all off."

David nodded. It was beginning to make sense. Actually, it wasn't too far from what he'd had in mind. Except that he'd been trying to get the kidnappers to think that Blair and all the rest of them were too cute and appealing to be bumped off. Amanda's idea was to make them think that Blair was too holy.

"You see why Janie mustn't know about it, don't you?" Amanda asked, and after he'd thought about it, David did. Wow, did he ever! Considering what Janie had made out of the King Tut plan, he hated to think what would happen if she started pretending she was taking part in a miracle. They'd wind up with something like Joan of Arc made into a Disney TV special—with Janie as Joan, of course. "But what will we do about her?" he asked.

"Well, it's not going to be easy, but I was thinking that if she thinks Blair and you and I really have seen the vision, and she knows she hasn't, at least she'll let us be—well—in charge of it, and she won't be so quick to start adding all sorts of fancy details. If she thinks it's just some kind of group "let's pretend," she'll just have to pretend bigger and better than anyone else.

David couldn't help cringing at the thought. "But she'll have to do the translating," he said. "She'll have to be the one to tell the kidnappers about what's happened and what we've seen. Won't it ruin it if she tells them that she hasn't seen it?"

"I don't see why. Not everybody can see visions, even real ones, I guess. Besides, I'll bet she tells them she's seen it too, just so she won't feel left out. But if she thinks that we've really seen it and she hasn't, she won't be so apt to get carried away."

"But what about Blair? We'll have to get him to say he's seen it."

"David," Amanda said in her familiar "how-can-you-be-so-dumb" tone of voice, "Blair's already seen it. At least he thinks he has. He dreamed it, and he thought it was real. And if we encourage him to think it was real, he will. He just won't know the difference."

"I don't think it's that he doesn't know the difference," David said. "He just doesn't think the difference is important."

"Well, whatever. Anyway, do you have any good ideas about how we might get started?"

They began immediately to work out all the details—who would say they'd seen it first, and what the other one would do, and what they'd get the little kids to do. They'd been planning for quite a while when David became aware of a sizzling noise that seemed to be coming from the kids hideout in the corner. He tiptoed over and peeked behind the boxes, and there were Janie and Esther and Blair squatting down in a tight little circle. Janie was whispering away like crazy. When she saw David looking at them, she said, "Go away. We're making plans, and you can't listen."

David went away thinking that Janie was only getting even for being left out of Amanda's plan. He should have known better. He should have known that whatever Janie was doing, it wasn't ever safe to think of it as "only" anything.

seventeen

David wasn't at all sure he liked Amanda's plan to have a fake miracle, but on the other hand, the time was getting shorter and shorter until the kidnappers would have to come to a decision about what to do with their captives. And if there was any chance their decision could be influenced in the right direction, it was certainly worth a try.

The first step was just to tell the little kids that they'd seen the Blue Lady. They'd decided to start out that way partly for practice in pretending—or lying, if you wanted to look at it that way—and partly to get the kids in the right frame of mind for what was going to come next. And the next step would be to actually pretend they were seeing something while the kids were watching.

Amanda started it. She waited until the kids had all been asleep and then, when they woke up, she told them that while they were asleep she and David had seen something very strange. She made her voice say that what she was about to tell them was very serious and important. Then she waited until she was sure she had their full attention. David couldn't help admiring her technique. She was acting as if she were trying to think of just the right way to tell them something terribly important and significant, while the kids got more and more curious and impatient.

"What was it, for heaven's sake?" Janie said. "What did you see?"

"Well," Amanda said finally, "after you and the twins had gone to sleep, David and I were sitting on my cot talking, when all of a sudden I noticed this strange sort of glow over there in the corner of the room."

"Strange sort of what?" Esther asked.

"Glow. Like a light. And right in the middle of the light there was—well, it was like a lady in a long robe. Standing over there on the box by the wall."

Blair was listening intently. "With a blue thing?" he asked, making a motion like something over his head and shoulders.

"Yes," Amanda said. "She had this long blue veil-like thing over her head, and her robe was white, I think, and her hands . . ." she paused, looking at Blair.

"Like this?" Blair asked, holding his hands together as if he were praying. "Her hands were like this?"

"Yes," Amanda said, "her hands were like this." She put her palms together and fixed her face so that it looked very sweet and sad. It was not an expression that David, or anyone else probably, had ever seen on Amanda's face before. He got so interested in what she was doing, he almost forgot about his own part—until Janie said, "You saw her, too, David?"

"Huh?" he said. "Me? Uh—yeah. I saw her, too. Just like Amanda said." And he did the bit with his hands and eyes. The looking down sadly at his folded hands came in handy, because it kept him from having to look directly at anybody—particularly at Blair, because he had a feeling that if he looked right at Blair he would blow it for sure. Blair would know that he was lying.

When Amanda had finished, no one said anything for quite a long time. Janie went over to the box in the corner and looked all around it. Then she came partway back and stopped and turned very quickly and looked at the box again. Blair was watching Janie, and for a while Esther did too, but then she started wandering off toward the table.

"Esther," Amanda said. "Weren't you listening? Didn't you hear about David and me seeing the Blue Lady?"

"Sure," she said. "I heard you. But I already knew about it. Blair already told me all about her." She went to the table and started stacking the dirty dishes and brushing at the table with her hands. "It's very dirty in here," she said. "Janie, why don't you tell those kidnappers it's too dirty in here?" Esther didn't seem to have premonitions about a lot of things, the way Blair did, but sometimes she seemed to where food was concerned. Just a few minutes later, the door opened and Gino came down the steps carrying the tray.

According to Amanda and David's plan, the next step was going to be actually seeing the vision while the kids were watching. *Then* they were going to suggest to Janie that she should tell the kidnappers about what was happening. But they should have known Janie wouldn't need that much encouragement. Gino had hardly reached the table when Janie began about the Blue Lady. She even acted it all out for Gino, running across the room and climbing up on the box and posing, to show the way the lady had been standing. It seemed as if she were doing a pretty good job of it, but it would have been more effective if Esther hadn't kept interrupting.

"Janie." Esther kept following her around and tugging at her. "Janie, tell him to bring us a dish cloth and some soapy water." And a little later while Janie was still posing on the box, she started whining about a broom and dustpan, and this time because Janie was out of reach, she started tugging at the kidnapper's jacket.

Without being able to see his expression, it was hard to tell for sure; but it seemed as if Gino was really impressed by what Janie was telling him. At least, he seemed to be giving her his full attention, except, of course, while Esther was tugging at him. When Janie said that Amanda and David and Blair had all seen the vision, the dark eyes in the masked face turned to stare at each of them, making David feel very uncomfortable. When Janie finally finished telling everything, Gino gathered up the dirty dishes and put them on the tray without saying anything to

Janie at all; but when he was halfway up the stairs, he stopped and turned around and asked her something.

"Sì," Janie said. "Anch'io."

He turned then quickly and looked back at the box by the wall, and David got the impression that he might have stood there looking for quite a while, except that just then Esther started demanding that Janie ask him if he had a vacuum cleaner.

It was very hard to tell what effect the whole thing had had on the kidnapper. After he had gone, David and Amanda questioned Janie very carefully about what had been said, and it seemed as if she had told it pretty much the way they'd told it to her, without adding too many of her own special touches. Except that when David asked her what Gino had said just before he went out she said, "Oh, he just asked me if I'd seen the Blue Lady, too."

"Oh," David nodded, but then suddenly something dawned on him. "Wait a minute," he said. "Doesn't 'anch'io' mean 'me too'?"

Janie rolled her eyes thoughtfully. "Well," she said. "Not exactly 'me too.' It's more like—"

"Janie," David said sternly. "It does, too. I remember now. So how come you told him you saw the Blue Lady, too?"

"Well—everybody else has, so I just thought I probably would too, as soon as I got a chance."

"You know, I wouldn't be at all surprised," Amanda said in her most sarcastic tone of voice.

Amanda seemed to feel that Janie, with Esther's

help, had pretty much blown the whole miracle thing, but David wasn't so sure. A little while later, when Gino came back with a bunch of cleaning stuff, a broom and dustpan and a bucket of soapy water for Esther, David thought it was a good sign. Amanda thought it was just the opposite, that it meant he'd been more impressed by Esther's attack of cleanliness than by Janie's miracle.

"I don't know if there's any use going on with it," Amanda said. "He probably didn't believe any of it for a minute. After all, if we'd just witnessed a miracle, would Esther have been running around talking about vacuum cleaners, for heaven's sake?"

"I don't know," David said. "He's been around Esther long enough to know the way she is when she gets an idea into her head. Like the way she was about the scrambled eggs the other day. It seems to me he probably realizes by now that when Esther sets her mind on something, it would take a lot more than a miracle to shake it loose."

Amanda sighed. "Well, maybe," she said. "I guess we might as well do the next part anyway, as long as we've gone this far."

However, they did decide to wait for an hour or two, since it seemed likely that miracles weren't apt to happen every few minutes. When Amanda thought that enough time had gone by, she told David to get ready, and then she began. At that particular moment Blair and Janie were watching the ants, and Esther was sweeping up a cloud of dust near the foot

176

of the stairs; but when Amanda said, "Look!" her voice was so dramatic they all stopped what they were doing and stared at her.

She was standing stiffly with one arm at her side and the other straight out in front of her, pointing at the wall above the box where Blair had seen the Blue Lady. The surprised expression on her face looked stiff too, as if it had been frozen there. The little kids looked at her, and then Janie and Blair ran out from behind the junk pile so they could see what she was pointing at. Then it was time for David to do his part.

Getting up off his cot he went over beside Amanda and said, "I see her, I see her, too." It came out sounding so phony that he couldn't help wincing —like a robot talking or somebody reading out of a first grade primer. But the little kids didn't seem to notice. They were all staring at the corner. Very slowly and dramatically, Amanda got down on her knees, and as soon as the kids noticed what she had done, they got down on their knees, too. So David knelt, even though it made him feel phonier than ever. The whole thing was making him feel very uncomfortable—without knowing exactly why. He felt relieved when, after what seemed a very long time, Amanda sighed and got to her feet.

"I didn't see anything," Esther said. "How come I didn't see anything?"

"Is she gone? Is she gone, Amanda?" Janie asked.

"Yes," Amanda said. "She's gone now, but maybe she'll come back again. I think maybe she wants to tell us something."

"What? What does she want to tell us?" Janie asked, but Amanda didn't answer. Instead she drifted back to her cot and sat down on it, looking kind of spaced-out and glassy-eyed. David and Janie and Esther followed her. Janie and Esther were still asking all sorts of questions, and it wasn't until several minutes later that someone noticed what Blair was doing.

Blair was still kneeling in the center of the cellar staring intently at the corner, and when David spoke to him, he didn't seem to hear. They all started toward him, and then, without anyone suggesting it, they all stopped.

David hadn't really noticed before how the one dim bulb in its metal shade cast a narrow cone of brighter light directly beneath it. But now Blair was kneeling in the exact center of the cone of light, so that there seemed to be a circle of radiance all around him. His head was tilted back, and there was a brightness about his hair and face that stood out in sharp contrast to the dim, dingy room. David caught his breath. Amanda's elbow poked his ribs, and she started to whisper something, but just then Blair's strange smile faded and he got quickly to his feet. Running across the room to the box, he looked all around it the way he had done before. Then he walked slowly back past the rest of them without saying anything, or even noticing that they were staring at him, and climbed up on his cot.

"Wow," Amanda whispered. "If we could only get him to do that when the kidnappers are here." Going over to the cot she said, "Blair. Blair, honey." He rolled over on his back and looked up at her. His eyes were wide open and enormous, but it was somehow as if he still wasn't seeing—at least not in the same way that other people did. He was looking towards Amanda, but his expression was shut off and private. David had seen Blair look that way before, so he wasn't at all surprised when he reached up and pulled the pillow down over his face and wouldn't let Amanda take it away.

eighteen

"Why couldn't they have come a few minutes ago," Amanda said. Both Gino and Pietro were coming down the stairs, and it couldn't have been more than a half an hour since they'd staged their miracle—and Blair had knelt in the circle of light.

"I wonder what they're here for this time," David said.

The two kidnappers looked the same as always —black-masked and leather-jacketed—but they were acting strangely. They came partway down and then sat on the stairs, talking together in low voices. The smallest one, Gino, seemed to be doing most of the talking. When he suddenly gestured towards the box in the corner, David glanced at Amanda and caught her doing the same to him. She raised her eyebrows in a "what-do-you-know?" expression. The kidnappers went on sitting there for such a long time, talking sometimes and sometimes just watching, that the little kids seemed to forget about them and went back to what they were doing. Janie had been building something out of pieces of wood, and Blair was helping Esther clean house by holding the dustpan for her while she swept. It wasn't until they'd been sitting there for a long time, that Gino called to Janie.

"Come on, David," Amanda said. "I want to be in on this," and she went over and stood next to Janie at the foot of the stairs.

As soon as Pietro asked Janie the first question, David was able to guess by the tone of his voice and the few words that he recognized, what his attitude was going to be. It was obvious that he was questioning Janie about the Blue Lady thing, and also that he was making it clear that he didn't really believe a word of it.

Janie answered him and went on answering until Amanda poked her. "What did he say? What are you telling him?" she asked.

"He wants to know if any of us had seen anymore visions, and I told him yes. I said that all of us, except maybe Esther, saw the Blue Lady again just a little while ago."

"Tell them about Blair," Amanda whispered. "Tell them that Blair is the one who saw her first and that he's the one that sees her better than the rest of us. Tell him about what Blair did when he—when we all saw the vision."

Janie talked to the two kidnappers again, and then they talked to each other, and after a while the one called Pietro told Janie to call Blair. So Janie did, and Blair very carefully handed the full dustpan to Esther and came to the stairs, looking very solemn and a little scared.

Pietro barked a question at him, and Janie

181

translated, "Did you see a vision of the Blessed Mother?"

Blair looked questioningly over his shoulder at David. His eyes were huge and frightened. David put his arm across Blair's shoulders.

"Tell them, Blair," he said softly.

"I—I saw the Blue Lady," Blair whispered.

"Dove?" Pietro asked.

"Where?" Janie said.

"There," Blair said, pointing towards the box in the corner. Then he ducked his head bashfully and leaned against David. The kidnappers' owlish eyes stared at him out of their black wool faces.

"Come on, Blair, honey," Amanda said, taking his hand and starting to pull him towards the center of the room. David grabbed his other hand and held on, glaring at Amanda.

"Leave him alone," he whispered fiercely.

"David! Let go. Do you want to ruin everything," Amanda hissed.

Against his better judgement, David let go, and Amanda led Blair to the spot under the light where he had been before and pushed him down on his knees. David was following close behind, feeling terribly worried without knowing exactly why, and Janie followed David. The kidnappers came down off the stairs and joined them, forming a circle around the kneeling Blair. Everyone stared at Blair, and he stared back at them with big, scared eyes, twisting his head back and forth as he looked from one to the other. He looked, David thought angrily, more like a frightened baby bird than a holy person seeing a vision, and it was all Amanda's fault for trying to make Blair a part of something phony.

"Look, Blair. Look over there," Amanda was whispering, pointing at the box, and Blair looked for a minute, but then he jumped up and ran to David and hid his face against David's stomach. Amanda came after him and started to pull him away again, but he held onto David and said, "No, no, no. I don't want to. Nobody's there. Nobody's there now."

"Cosa ha detto?" Gino said and when Janie told him in Italian, Pietro shrugged, made a snorting noise and walked away. Turning to watch Pietro, everyone seemed to notice at once that the door at the top of the stairs was standing wide open.

Pietro ran halfway up the stairs, turned and looked frantically around the cellar, yelling a question at Janie. The question was about Esther, and you didn't have to know Italian to know what it was, because Esther had disappeared. Pushing David roughly out of the way, Gino dashed past him into the corner behind the junk pile and then around it and into the toilet room. Then he ran past David again and took the stairs three at a time, past Pietro and out the door. A second later Pietro had disappeared, too.

"Wow!" Janie said. "What will they do to Tesser for running away?"

The three of them stared at each other and then back up the stairs to where the door was still standing wide open—and then all at once, they were running, too, jostling each other on the stairs and then bursting through into a large, cluttered room. No one was in sight, but across the room another door swung partly open, and through it David saw sunlight, and in the distance a bit of tree-covered hillside. He ran again, out the door and into dazzling light. Almost blinded by the sudden brilliance, he came to a sudden stop, and Amanda and Janie crashed into him from behind.

"Look!" Amanda cried, pointing. On the other side of a large cleared area, Esther was standing beside a big metal barrel. Still holding the dustpan over the barrel, she seemed rooted to the spot, a startled expression on her face, as Gino and Pietro rapidly bore down on her, their heavy boots thundering on the hard-packed earth. Then, coming suddenly to life, she let out a terrified wail, threw the dustpan in the air, and turned to run.

"Run, Tesser, run," Janie shrieked, and a second later she was running, too, in the opposite direction. David ran one step after Janie, remembered Blair, alone in the cellar, and stopped, and Amanda ran into him again.

"Run, you idiot. We're free," Amanda said, shoving him out of her way, and then they were both running at top speed, toward the tree-covered hillside.

When they reached the trees, they stopped to look back, in time to see that Esther had been caught. One of the kidnappers was carrying her back toward the house. The other was running again—straight for them.

"Scatter," Amanda gasped. "I'll go this way," and she crashed off through the brush, and David, feeling terrified—not just for himself but for Blair left behind, and Esther caught, and Janie somewhere in the forest—ran on alone. But not alone for long, because the clomping, thundering footsteps behind him got louder and closer as he ducked around trees, slid down steep inclines, jumped a small creek and scrambled up the other side. He was on level ground again when he jumped a fallen tree trunk, stumbled, and as he regained his balance, a hand clamped down on his shoulder and he was spun around to stare into the angry eyes of Pietro.

David went quietly. A few minutes later he was shoved through the cellar door and it was slammed and locked behind him. The only other person in the room was Esther, who was standing at the foot of the stairs crying. She wasn't making much noise, but tears were pouring out of her eyes and streaming down her face and dripping off her chin onto her bathrobe.

"Oh David," she gasped when he stumbled down the steps, still staggering from Pietro's angry shove, "I'm so glad you came back." Throwing her arms around him before he had time to completely regain his balance, she tripped them both and they wound up stepping on each other's feet, kicking each other's shins, and finally sitting on the floor.

185

"Glad," David said angrily, rubbing his shin "What are you glad about? You should have been hoping I'd get away so I could go for help."

Wiping her face with both hands, Esther stared at him. He must have looked very angry because she started to cry all over again. "I'm sorry, David. I'm sorry I was glad. But—but I was all al-o-o-ne."

"No you weren't. Blair's here." He started to look around for Blair, but at that moment the door banged open again and then shut, and Amanda was coming down the steps. David and Esther rushed to meet her.

She was frightened and angry and so out of breath that it was a long time before she could say anything at all. There was mud on her jacket and jeans, and when she held out her hands, they saw that the palms were scratched and bleeding. "I'd have gotten away if I hadn't fallen down," she managed to gasp at last. "Right after we got to the edge of the clearing, I fell down so hard it knocked the wind out of me and by the time I'd gotten up Gino was right behind me." She sat down at the table, buried her face in her arms, and her shoulders shook with angry sobs. David stood around watching helplessly. After a while she raised her head and looked around. "Where's Janie?" she asked. "And Blair?"

"I guess they haven't caught Janie yet," David said. "I don't know where Blair is. He must be here someplace." David was sure Blair hadn't come with them when they dashed up the stairs, but he'd always had a way of hiding when things got frightening or unpleasant. David looked behind the junk pile and in the toilet room and was just checking under the beds when the door opened again. They'd caught Janie, too.

Both Gino and Pietro were coming down the stairs with Janie between them. Each of them held one of her arms tightly, and by the way they kept their eyes on her, you'd have thought they were leading a dangerous animal instead of a seven-year-old girl. Near the bottom of the stairs, they looked at each other, nodded, turned her loose and stepped back. Janie was red-faced and tousled, and her eyes looked bright and dangerous. Pietro's mask was askew and the front of his leather jacket was smeared with mud. Gino was rubbing his hand.

"Janie," David said aghast. "What happened?"

"I fought," Janie said and her voice quavered dramatically, "like a wild thing. I kicked and scratched and bit." She looked at Gino who was examining his thumb. "I think I bit him on the same thumb."

"On the same thumb as what?" Amanda asked.

"As I bit him on last time—when they kidnapped us."

Pietro straightened his mask and brushed off the front of his jacket and looked around the room.

"*Dov' e Blair?*" he asked.

"Where's Blair?" Janie said.

"I don't know," David said. "I was just looking for him when you came in. He must be here somewhere." But when they all, including the two kidnappers, had looked for several minutes, it became clear that he probably wasn't. There weren't that many places to hide in the cellar, and Blair wasn't in any of them. Although he couldn't imagine Blair doing it, David finally had to conclude that Blair had somehow managed to sneak out of the cellar without being seen by anyone.

He supposed that he should be glad. As long as one of them was still free, there was certainly more chance of rescue, even if the free person was Blair, who usually reacted to trouble by curling up in a corner somewhere and sucking his thumb. David tried not to imagine Blair wandering around in the forest alone and lost and maybe not finding anyone before it got dark. He was trying so hard not to think about it that he couldn't think about anything else, until suddenly he became aware of something that felt like a wave of terror. Everyone in the cellar seemed frozen into postures of listening, like a bunch of animals with their ears cocked towards a strange sound. From somewhere not far away, and rapidly getting closer, a sputtering, roaring motor noise was approaching the hideout. A second later Gino and Pietro were scrambling up the stairs and out the door.

"Wow!" Janie said. "They're scared."

"Yeah, I got that feeling, too," David said. "They must be afraid of what Red Mask will do when he finds out about what happened—and about Blair being gone."

Outside the motor noise got louder and louder and then, quite nearby, sputtered into silence.

"Do you suppose they'll tell him?" David asked.

"They'll have to. He'll find out sooner or later that Blair isn't here," Amanda said.

David sighed. "Yeah, I suppose so." Feeling desperately worried—about Blair and Red Mask and everything—David went to his cot and threw himself on it face down—and a split second later he was sitting up pawing frantically at the covers. Blinking sleepily, Blair uncurled himself from a tight little ball in the center of the sag in the cot. "Ouch," he said. "You squashed me, David."

"Hey," Janie said. "He was there all the time. How'd you do that, Blair?"

"I hid," Blair said. "And then I went to sleep."

"Do it again, Blair," Esther said. "Let's see how you did it."

Blair curled up again in the sag in the middle of the cot, and with the covers bunched up over him, no one would ever have guessed there was anyone there.

They were still fussing over Blair, getting used to the idea that he wasn't gone after all, when the kidnappers came back—all three of them. Red Mask came down the stairs first, loud and angry as always, with the other two trailing along behind. Blair was standing by the table, but Red Mask ignored him and immediately told Janie about a new ransom note he wanted Amanda to write. All the time Red Mask was dictating, Gino and Pietro stood behind him near the stairs, leaning limply on the bannisters and staring at Blair.

nineteen

"I don't think they told him anything," Amanda said.

"Well," David said, "they obviously didn't tell him about Blair being gone, because he didn't seem a bit surprised to see him. But they might have told him about us escaping."

"Did he mention the escape, Janie?" Amanda asked. "Did he warn us not to try it again or anything?"

Janie shook her head. "No. All he talked about was how knew your father was lying to him about not having enough money. And how you had to convince him that he'd better get the money—or else."

David shivered. He'd heard Janie's translation of the things Red Mask wanted Amanda to put in the letter. Janie had told Amanda to write that if her father didn't get enough money, Amanda and the others would soon be *"morto."* Janie hadn't translated *"morto."* Instead she had looked at Esther and Blair, raised her eyebrows significantly, and said, "Just put *morto*. Your father will know what means." Esther and Blair hadn't seemed to know what it meant, but David did.

He had to swallow hard before he could get his voice working to ask Janie, "Did he say when? Did he set any deadline?"

"No," Janie shook her head. "He just said *presto*—soon."

David sighed. "If we just had a little more time," he said to Amanda. "We were just beginning to get somewhere with—" He nodded towards Blair. "You know—with the plan."

"I have a plan, too," Janie said, but nobody paid much attention.

"Were is right," Amanda said. "We *were* getting somewhere until Esther's big escape. But that really blew it. I was beginning to think we were getting to Gino, and maybe Pietro, too. I was really thinking they might help us get away or something. But then Esther had to go and start everybody escaping." Amanda shrugged hopelessly. "Do you think they're going to care what happens to any of us after having to chase us all over the country, wearing themselves out and falling into ditches and"—she stopped to glare at Janie—"and getting their thumbs nearly bitten off."

"I *wasn't* escaping," Esther said. "I just went upstairs to look for a wastepaper basket to put the dust in, and there wasn't any in their house, and then I saw a garbage can out in the yard. I was going to come right back, only they went and ran at me and scared me."

"Great!" Amanda said. "Just great! What a bunch to get kidnapped with! She has a perfectly wonderful chance to get away, and all she can think about is emptying a dustpan."

Esther looked hurt—and puzzled. "But you just said—" she started.

"Never mind, Tesser," David said. "It wasn't your fault. None of it was your fault." He turned to Amanda. "The thing is," he said, "if they didn't tell Red Mask about the escape, it might mean they are still a little bit on our side. Like maybe they didn't want him to know because he'd be so angry at us."

"Or at them," Amanda said. "I think they didn't tell him because they're scared to death of him, too. And if he knew they'd been careless enough to leave the door open when they came down here, he'd really be furious—at them. That's probably the only reason they didn't tell him."

"Well, maybe," David said. But just then another idea began to take shape in the back of his mind. "Hey, wait a minute. I just thought of something. You probably didn't notice because you were busy writing the letter to your father, but while Red Mask was telling Janie what you were supposed to say, Gino and Pietro were standing over there by the stairs, and they were just *staring* at Blair as if—" Suddenly remembering that Janie wasn't supposed to know about the "miracle" plan, David stopped. "Uh-Janie," he said. "Why don't you go and—see what the ants are doing?"

Janie glared at him. "All right for you, David," she said. "You'll be sorry. I won't tell you my plan, either. Come on, Blair. Tesser. Let's go talk about our plan."

While the little kids were busy whispering in the corner, David told Amanda the interesting idea that had occurred to him. He described how Gino and Pietro had stared at Blair in such a strange way, it was almost as if they thought there'd been something —well, almost supernatural about his disappearance and then sudden reappearance.

Amanda caught on right away. "Yeah," she said. "If we don't tell them about finding him in the bed—maybe we can say that we just happened to look up and all of a sudden there he was again— kneeling in the corner near the Blue Lady's box."

"Yeah, like that. Only there's one problem."

Amanda nodded. "Janie," she said.

"Janie knows where we really found him. We'll have to tell her about what we're trying to do—since she has to be the one to tell them about it."

"Well, maybe not," Amanda said. "Maybe you could just get Janie to tell them about his suddenly appearing near the box without telling her exactly what we've been trying to do. Maybe if you promise that we'll tell her all about it right afterwards, if she does a good job, she won't be so apt to hokey it all up."

So David agreed to try. He called Janie out from behind the junk pile and explained what they wanted done. At first she said she wouldn't unless they'd tell her all about their plan; but when David asked her to do it for him and promised that he and Amanda would tell her all the rest of the plan very soon afterwards, she said okay. It wasn't as if he was lying to her. There was a chance—a slight chance anyway—that the plan might work soon, and Gino and Pietro might set them all free. Then he would be able to tell Janie all about it. But for now he only told Janie what they wanted her to tell Gino and Pietro about how they'd all been sitting around worrying about where Blair was, when all of a sudden they heard something, and they looked up and there he was, kneeling in front of the box. Janie was a fast learner. After hearing David tell it just once, she went through it again in English, almost word for word—and then rattled it all off in Italian, just to show him how she was going to do it. Then there was nothing more to do but wait until Gino and Pietro came in again—without Red Mask.

It must have been shortly after that conversation with Janie that David noticed the belt to his bathrobe was missing. In fact he was still looking for it when Pietro came in alone, with the last meal of the day, and David forgot all about the belt. Everything seemed to work out fine. Pietro actually set it all up himself by asking Janie where Blair had been while they were all looking for him. So then, of course, Janie launched into the mysterious reappearance story, and David was able to understand enough of the words to tell that she was doing a good job. She even went over and knelt down in front of the box to demonstrate where Blair had been when they

194

first noticed him. With his face covered by the hood, it was hard to tell for sure, but from the thoughtful way Pietro put the food on the table, it looked as if he'd been pretty impressed by Janie's story.

Not long after Pietro left the cellar, someone left the hideout by motorcycle. David noticed especially, because it occurred to him that it was probably someone taking the latest ransom note to be mailed or delivered to Amanda's father. He wondered which one of the kidnappers had taken it. Dinner had just been served so the day was over, and it was usually about this time that Red Mask came to the hideout and Gino and Pietro went away. However he'd only heard one motorcycle start up, and it didn't seem likely that Red Mask would allow Gino or Pietro to deliver a ransom note.

There was one other thing that happened that evening that might have given David some warning if he'd been a little more alert. Just as the little kids were getting into bed, Janie asked David if he thought Red Mask was still the one who stayed at the hideout at night.

"I don't know," David said. "I suppose so. Why?"

"Oh, I just wondered," Janie said, and that was all.

It was probably an hour or two later—David had been asleep for quite a while—when he suddenly woke up. He lay there for a minute wondering what had awakened him. Either it had been a dream, or he had heard the motorcycle noise again. He wondered sleepily about who was coming and going so late at night and then, just as he was about to go back to sleep, he heard something else. A soft scraping noise that came from not far away. His eyes flew open.

At first he didn't see anything, but then something under the table moved and caught his eye—and there was Janie. She seemed to be crouching down below the table, hanging onto the table leg with both hands.

Sitting up in bed he whispered, "Janie. What are you doing?"

"Nothing." She got up quickly and tiptoed toward him. "I couldn't sleep, so I decided to play a little game by myself. I was just playing a game about—being a bear and under the table was my cave. I was just playing it was winter, and I was getting ready to hibernate and—"

"Janie," David said wearily, "shut up and go to bed."

"Okay," Janie said agreeably—much too agreeably, he realized afterwards. "Okay. I'll hibernate in bed."

David sighed and turned over and went back to sleep. It must have been a very sound sleep because the next thing he knew he was sitting straight up in bed, wondering frantically if the world were coming to an end. The cellar was full of sound, an incredible thumping, crashing, screaming noise, loud enough to wake the dead. The first thing he thought was that there'd been an earthquake and the hideout had fallen in on them, so the first place he looked was up—but the ceiling was still there, and so was the cellar—but in the midst of it Janie and Esther and Blair were pounding on a water bucket with sticks and screaming at the top of their lungs.

Oh, he thought, it's only Janie and Esther and Blair pounding on a bucket and screaming. And then, a second later—what on earth are they doing that for? He was just jumping out of bed to make them stop when the cellar door crashed open and Red Mask appeared at the top of the stairs in just his undershorts and red mask. For one awful moment he stared down at Janie and the twins, and then he started to shout and run down the stairs. An instant later he lurched forward and launched himself into space. Shooting down the rest of the way head-first, Red Mask landed at the bottom of the stairs with a terrible thud.

What happened next must not have taken more than a few seconds, but it seemed, somehow, that everything shifted into a weird kind of slow motion, so that there was time to see what was about to happen and to think, Oh no, this can't be happening, before it actually did. It seemed as if Red Mask was lying stretched out on the floor moaning for a long time before David noticed what Esther and Janie and Blair were doing—before he saw they had stopped pounding on the water bucket and were getting ready to start pounding on Red Mask.

Janie was yelling, "Tie his feet, Blair. Hit him hard, Esther."

When he realized what they meant to do, all David could think about was what Red Mask would do to them for hitting him—and he lunged forward in time to grab Janie's table leg just before it crashed down on Red Mask's head. As he jerked it away from her and pulled her away from Red Mask, there was a weird everlasting instant during which he watched Blair wrapping a bathrobe belt around one of Red Mask's ankles, and Esther whacking him on the back with a piece of wood.

"Hit him, David. Knock him out!" Janie yelled, and David raised the table leg and looked down at Red Mask's head, but somehow he couldn't do it. He went on standing there while the kidnapper shook his hooded head and then pushed himself to a sitting position. Then he looked around, and making a kind of growling noise, he staggered to his feet, his swinging arms toppling Blair and Esther like rag dolls. David retreated backwards across the room, and Red Mask came after him.

Towering over David like a huge half-naked giant, Red Mask kept coming, and every step was, for David, a long, distinct and vivid eternity. And then Red Mask reached out and grabbed the club, and David hung onto it desperately and was jerked and tossed as Red Mask tried to shake him loose. David's grip was weakening, the club was being torn from his fingers, when something hit Red Mask from behind so violently that he crashed into David, and David crashed into the wall behind him; and for a little while there was nothing at all except the struggle to get some air back into his lungs.

As David's eyes and lungs started working again, he was aware first of all of Janie, jumping up and down and making a noise like a cheerleader at a football game—and then of two extra people who were sitting on top of Red Mask tying his wrists and ankles with bathrobe belts. The two people looked like teen-aged boys, and although they weren't wearing masks, they were wearing boots and black leather jackets. When they ran out of belts, they got up off Red Mask and the tallest one said something to Janie.

"Pietro says we'd better get out of here fast," Janie said—and they did.

twenty

For almost half an hour David had been sitting on the terrace wall enjoying the view and thinking. What he had been thinking about was how there could be times in a person's life when, for a little while, everything seemed to be just about perfect. It was that kind of a day. That kind of a week, actually. And two days ago it had even turned amazingly warm for November, as if Nature was trying to do something special for the occasion, too.

Besides thinking, he'd been noticing how the clear blue of the sky lightened to turquoise near the tops of the hills and how the vines on the walls of the villa were turning to gold and brilliant red, and how the Swedish students who lived across the courtyard were taking advantage of the unexpected weather to get a last minute layer of suntan. It was especially interesting to notice that Swedish people sometimes sunbathed with less clothing on than you might expect.

Besides thinking and watching the interesting view, the other thing David was doing was waiting for Amanda to come back from Florence. For the last two days Amanda had been staying with her father in Florence, but today he was to catch a plane back to California, and Dad and Molly had driven into the city to bring Amanda back to the villa.

"Hey, David." It was Janie's voice, and he looked up to see her leaning out of her window on the second floor.

"What do you want?" he called before he realized that she didn't really want anything, except perhaps attention.

"Hi!" she called again, even louder. "Hi, David."

The Swedish girls looked up and waved at Janie, and she waved back. "David," she yelled, "I'm coming down." She disappeared for a minute, and then she was back leaning out the window again, but this time without her tee shirt. "I'll be right down," she called. "Here I come."

David sighed and went back to admiring the view, and a few seconds later Janie came out of the front door wearing nothing but a pair of shorts—not that it made much difference in Janie's case. She skipped across the courtyard, waving at David, and on over to where the Swedish girls were sunbathing. After she'd stood around talking to them for a while, one of them spread out a towel for her, and she lay down beside them and went on talking. They were too far away for David to be sure, but he supposed they were talking English, since the Swedish girls all spoke some English, and as far as he knew Janie didn't speak any Swedish—not yet anyway. He could hear enough, though, to tell that Janie was doing most of the talking. Now and then one of the girls seemed to be asking her a question, and every once in a while they would all laugh. David stayed where he was, watching the view and the beautiful day, and the road that went down to the village, and a while later Janie got up and came over to the terrace wall.

"What are you doing, David?" she asked. "I've been sunbathing."

"I'm just waiting," he said, "for Dad and Molly and Amanda to come back from Florence. What were you saying to the Swedish girls? What were you telling them about? You remember what Dad said about talking so much about the kidnapping."

"I wasn't talking so much," Janie said. "They were asking me questions."

"What kind of questions?"

"Well," Janie rolled her eyes thoughtfully, "mostly about my plan. They wanted to know about my plan."

David sighed again. Everyone had heard a great deal about Janie's plan. Everyone who'd gotten within earshot had heard over and over again about how she had taught the twins their part of the plan, and how she had swiped David's belt when he wasn't looking, and how after everyone was asleep she had tied the belt to the bannisters near the top of the stairs so that anyone coming down would trip over it, and how she woke up the twins and when they were all ready she said, "ready-set-go," and they began to beat on the bucket and scream. And then Esther was going to help her knock Red Mask out while Blair tied him up. Only David had interfered and spoiled it all, and everything would have turned out very badly, except that Gino and Pietro were still there, which she hadn't expected, but which turned out to be very lucky.

They'd been very lucky, all right. Now and then during the last week, David had given himself cold chills by thinking about just how terribly lucky they'd been. In between all the great times, being back with Dad and Molly, having their names and pictures in the papers, being on TV, and starting back to school where everyone made such a fuss that it almost got to be embarrassing, David had sometimes thought about how easily it might all have turned out very differently. How Gino and Pietro wouldn't have been there that late at night except that Red Mask had just returned from delivering the ransom note, so that instead of being home in bed as they usually were at that hour, they were just getting on their motorcycles when Janie and the twins started banging on the bucket.

But nobody talked much about what might have happened. What the papers told, and what everybody talked about, was how it all actually turned out. Everyone knew now about how the Lino boys had met Red Mask, who's real name was Alberto Scalione, who was a lot older and who had been in trouble with the law several times before; and how they had told him about the rich American girl who was a friend of their sister's. It looked now as if it had been Scalione who planned the kidnapping from the beginning—who'd found the deserted farmhouse and prepared the note that lured Amanda out of the house, and who planned the roundabout route that had made it seem that the hideout was a great distance from Valle, when in reality it hadn't been far away at all.

Everything had been in the papers. As a matter of fact, there'd been a lot of stuff in the papers that, in David's opinion, hadn't been all that necessary. Dad had said that in the beginning, when the children were still missing, the newspaper people had been very helpful and sympathetic; but since the rescue, they'd started printing some rather humorous articles, some of which David could have done without.

There'd been one about the kidnapping itself, about how the kidnappers had set out to capture one victim and had wound up with a lot more than they'd bargained for, that he could see real humor in. But there were others that dwelt on the fact that after the captives had been released, they'd managed to get themselves so thoroughly lost in the woods, they'd gone on being missing for several more hours. The articles had told about how, after the release, the Lino boys had turned themselves in, and led the police back to the hideout where Scalione was still lying on the floor tied up with bathrobe belts—and the whole mystery had been solved, with the minor exception of the fact that no one could locate the kidnap victims. Where they had actually been was in a rather small patch of woods near the hideout, and what they had been doing was going around in circles because of trying to plot a course by looking for moss on the sides of tree trunks.

The article had made it all sound rather amusing, and David could see now that it was, but it hadn't seemed particularly funny at the time. Not with Esther whining and Blair losing his clothes because Janie's plan had used up not only his bathrobe belt and shoe strings, but also the drawstring out of his pajama pants, and Janie and Amanda arguing about moss and tree trunks and which way they ought to be going. But then, they'd eventually stumbled on a farmhouse and been recognized and kissed and cried over by the farm woman, and soon afterwards they were back at the villa—with Dad and Molly and the Thatchers and everybody being hysterical with joy.

There was just one part of the whole thing that no one talked about very much, and that was Blair's dream. David and Amanda had talked it over, right after they got home, and decided they weren't going to bring it up, and after they explained it to Janie, she agreed not to bring it up, either. There were a lot of reasons. The main one was the effect the story might have on the Lino family. Gino and Pietro had tackled Red Mask and let the Stanleys loose and maybe even saved their lives; and if David and Amanda started going around saying that it had only turned out that way because they'd tricked Gino and

Pietro into believing that Blair had seen a vision—it wouldn't do anyone any good.

It certainly wouldn't do Gino and Pietro any good, or Ghita, their mother—or Marzia, who just as David had suspected hadn't had anything to do with the kidnapping at all.

And then, too, as Amanda pointed out, if everyone did start believing that Blair had been part of a miracle, it might turn out a lot like the movie she'd seen on TV, and that obviously wouldn't be good for Blair. Besides, David wasn't at all sure about what he, himself, believed about what Blair had seen in the corner of the cellar. Not long after they'd gotten back home, he'd tried to question Blair about it. He and Blair had been coming down the front stairs at the time, and they'd stopped at the landing with the statue of the Virgin.

"Blair," David had said, "did you really see the Blue Lady on the box in the cellar? I mean *really*, Blair."

Blair looked at the statue and then back at David. He pointed at the statue and said, "Don't you see that? Don't you see that Blue Lady, David?"

"Well, of course, I see that," David said.

"Is that really? Is that really the Blue Lady?"

"Well, it's really a statue," David said, feeling a little confused.

Blair nodded happily, looking as if he thought everything was all solved. "A dream is really," he said. "A dream is really a dream."

David sighed. "Look," he said, "we'd better

hurry up. I think it's time for dinner." And that had been the end of the investigation.

"Hey look. Here they come," Janie said, and David came out of the past to the terrace wall in the warm sunshine, and to Janie walking up and down the wall with her arms held out as if she were walking a tightrope. "Here comes Dad and Molly and Amanda." She jumped down off the wall and ran toward the gate that led into the courtyard. The car came through the gate, and Janie ran behind it, waving and yelling, all the way to the parking place on the lower terrace. David got off the wall and followed more slowly.

Amanda was getting out of the car wearing a new skirt and blouse that were very stylish and Italian-looking. She was hugging Janie when David came up, and then she turned loose of Janie and grabbed David and hugged him, too. She went off toward the house with one arm around Molly and the other around Janie.

"Wow!" David said. He'd never thought of Amanda as the hugging type, particularly not where he was concerned.

Dad laughed. "I know just what you mean," he said. "Some people seem to have done a bit of changing lately." He opened the trunk and began getting out groceries and other packages. "Here, David. Could you give me a hand with these?" he said.

"Well, in Amanda's case," David said, "I think part of it has to do with how she was feeling about her father." It was something David hadn't gotten around to discussing with his father, so while they carried in the groceries, he began to go into some of the things Amanda had told him about her father while they were in the cellar. About how she felt her father didn't love her—and what a difference it had made when she'd heard that he had come to Italy to try to save her, even though he couldn't get all the money the kidnappers wanted.

In the kitchen, Dad put water on the stove for coffee and sat down at the kitchen table, and David sat down, too. Dad was looking very thoughtful. "A good observation," he said at last, "and a reminder that I've needed from time to time in the past year. With her own father apparently indifferent, and Molly occupied with a new family, it's not surprising that Amanda has felt like getting even with the world, now and then."

Dad got up and made his coffee and got some cookies out of one of the sacks of groceries. Then he sat down and passed the cookies to David and said, "Yes, I think the whole Stanley family has learned some very important things. Molly and I were talking last night about how much we'd learned, not just about our own family, but about other people as well."

David knew what Dad was talking about. He'd already heard Dad and Molly telling about how much help and support other people had been during the terrible time when the children were missing. Not only the renters at the villa, but also lots of people from the village and farms, had tried to help in any way they could. Molly said the Italian people had been marvelous, and she didn't know how she and Dad could have lived through that awful time if it hadn't been for all the people who helped and sympathized.

"Speaking of learning," Dad said, "according to Ghita, Gino and Pietro have done a lot of learning, too. We stopped by to see her on our way into Florence this morning. You know how terrible it was for her when she heard her boys were involved in the kidnapping; but today she seemed to be almost her old cheerful self. She'd just heard that the court will probably be quite lenient with the boys, because of their ages and the testimony you and Amanda gave about their behavior at the end when the chips were down.

"But Ghita said it wasn't just the judge's decision that was making her feel so much better. She seems to think that her boys have developed a different attitude about a lot of things lately. Apparently they've worried her a lot in the last few years, but now she seems to think they're starting to become much more —well, as she expressed it, *'giudiziosi.'* "

"Giudiziosi?" David asked.

"Serious and responsible."

David nodded and after a moment shook his head—thinking of the poor Lino boys. He couldn't help feeling sorry for them. Of course, they had brought it all on themselves by taking up with crummy people and listening to bad advice, but they'd started paying for it almost from the beginning—from that first bitten thumb—and now, even with the judge being lenient, they still had a lot more paying to do.

As for Red Mask, there were times lately when David even felt a little sorry for him. The papers said that when the polizia had first found him, tied up in the bathrobe belts, he'd been kind of babbling, and recently they were saying that his trial was going to have to be postponed until he'd recovered from the nervous breakdown he'd been having. It was too bad, actually, but perhaps it was the kind of thing you had to expect if you went into something like kidnapping.

That night in the villa the whole family sat up late listening to Amanda tell about her visit with her father in Florence, and talking over things in general. The Thatchers were there, too, and everybody was in a great mood. They made a huge fire in the fireplace and then grilled steaks on the coals, and there was a lot of laughing and singing and kidding around, until a long time past everyone's regular bedtime.

Since the next day was Saturday, David was planning to sleep late; but practically before dawn Esther came through his room pushing her toy vacuum cleaner and making a loud whirring noise through her teeth, which was supposed to represent the vacuum cleaner motor. He'd just gotten through yelling at her to get out, when Blair wandered in looking for his shoe, and David had to wake up enough to tell him that he'd seen it under the kitchen table. Then just as he was about to get back to sleep, Janie came in and climbed up on the foot of his bed and announced that she'd finally found the part in *Isabella and the Secret of Holby House* about being hysterical with terror, and she was going to read it to him.

David sat up. "Forget it," he said. "I have to go to the bathroom."

"You can't," Janie said. "Amanda's got the door locked. I just tried."

David groaned and flopped back down on the bed and pulled the pillow over his head. Through the pillow he could hear Janie reading in a very hysterical tone of voice, and after a while he took the pillow off his head and listened because at least it was better than thinking about how badly he needed to go to the bathroom. He was just beginning to get involved in wondering what it was that Isabella was so hysterical about, when Janie stopped reading and listened. "I think Amanda came out," she said.

"Whew," David said, "what a relief." But before he could get untangled from the blankets, Janie threw down her book and dashed out the door. He could hear her yelling, "My turn. Me next. My turn," all the way down the hall until the bathroom door slammed shut behind her. He was already out of bed by then so he went to look out of the window, but that didn't help a bit because it had started to rain. So he sat down quickly on the bed to wait.

Wow, he thought. Rain. What happened to the

perfect weather? And while he was on that subject, what had happened to perfect in general? What had happened to everything being so perfect for the whole last week? For a moment he considered lying back down and pulling the pillow over his head again—but just then he heard Janie coming back down the hall.

Shooting out the door, he careened off the wall on the other side of the hall and got to the bathroom door just as Esther chugged through it with her vacuum cleaner. There wasn't time to argue, so he just picked her up, vacuum cleaner and all, and set her back down in the hall.

All the time he was in the bathroom he could hear her fussing at him outside the door. "Good-bye perfect," he muttered to himself. Everything was back to normal. Amanda had spent her normal couple of hours in the bathroom. Janie had been normally sneaky. And now Esther was doing her normal whine outside the door. But a moment later while he was splashing water on his face, another thought struck him and he grinned at himself in the mirror. Maybe perfect was over, but at least in the Stanley household, normal was hardly ever boring.

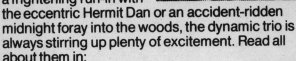

Tales of adventure through time and space
MADELEINE L'ENGLE

☐ **A WRINKLE IN TIME** $2.95 (49805-8)
It was a wild, stormy night when the unearthly visitor arrived to change the lives of Meg, her small brother Charles, and their scientist mother. A Newbery Medal winner.

☐ **A WIND IN THE DOOR** $2.50 (48761-7)
The forces of good and evil battle, through a day and night of terror, for Charles's life and the ultimate salvation of mankind.

☐ **A SWIFTLY TILTING PLANET** $3.25 (40158-5)
Charles, now fifteen, and the unicorn Gaudior undertake a perilous journey through time in a desperate attempt to stop the destruction of the world by the dictator Madog Branzillo.

YEARLING BOOKS

DANCING

If dancing holds a special magic for you, don't miss these charming stories. Set in England before you were born, they follow the amusing adventures of some *very* talented children.

——BALLET SHOES 41508-X-62 ....$3.50

——DANCING SHOES 42289-2-65 ....$3.25

——FAMILY SHOES 42479-8-24 ....$3.25

——MOVIE SHOES 45815-3-46 ....$3.25

——NEW SHOES 46304-1- $3.50

——SKATING SHOES 47731-X-43 ....$2.95

——THEATRE SHOES 48791-9-14 ....$3.25

——TRAVELING SHOES 48732-3-32 ....$2.95

Not available in Canada

by Noel Streatfeild